BETTER WITH BUTTER

Victoria Piontek

Scholastic Inc.

This book was originally published in hardcover by Scholastic Press in 2021.

All rights reserved. Published by Scholastic Inc., *Publishers since 1920*. SCHOLASTIC and associated logos are trademarks and/or registered trademarks of Scholastic Inc.

ISBN 978-1-338-66221-4

10 9 8 7 6 5 4 3 2 1   22 23 24 25 26

Printed in the U.S.A. 40
This edition first printing 2022

Book design by Keirsten Geise

FOR MY HERD: CLARICE, WILLIAM, GAVIN, AND DAVID

COWARDICE 101

It's not easy being a coward. In fact, it takes a lot of work to be afraid of everything. I have to *always* be on alert for things that *might* happen. Impending doom.

Catastrophes like: terminal illness, food poisoning, global warming, famine, earthquakes (I live near San Francisco), rising sea levels, species extinction, and that big island of plastic floating through the ocean. I know how I sound. But spend five seconds on the Internet, and it's all right there. For every tragic event I mentioned, there's a story to prove it *could* happen or *is* happening—that floating plastic island is real.

My parents say I'm too young for all these worries, but I can't help it. My mind just goes there. It whirls like one of those miserable spinning rides at amusement parks (a ride I would never go on because all that turning could trigger incurable vertigo), whipping up every possible tragic outcome.

Mom and Dad (and the school therapist) call my worries an anxiety disorder, but I call them armor. I mean, if something can happen, it will. That's what Murphy's Law is all about. (Google it. It's terrifying.) I need to be prepared.

Even when I'm not thinking of global, world-ending tragedies, I'm thinking of small worries—me-centric concerns. Things like: friends (not having any, having too many, losing the one I think I have), tests (especially math), flunking sixth grade, getting called on by the teacher, classroom presentations or (way worse) whole-school presentations, public humiliation (all kinds—unwanted crushes, wrong answers, tripping, falling . . . let your imagination run wild. I do).

The school therapist says I have a generalized anxiety disorder. That means I'm a free-range worrier, like an organic chicken. I basically worry just to worry. I'm supposed to work on it—do deep breathing exercises, practice mindfulness, journal, make fact-based charts, and logically explore my fears. But honestly, I'm afraid to; I might discover more things to worry about.

It's like my mind leapfrogs from one stomach-dropping terror to the next. Though, right now, I'm most concerned about my Famous Californian presentation. It's a BIG DEAL because it's the start of our public speaking unit that ends in the grand finale—the sixth-grade play. A huge, showstopping extravaganza that everyone at school PLUS parents, grandparents, brothers, and sisters (and probably distant relatives) show up to see. They even record it and upload it to the Internet, where it can be viewed over and over and over again until the end of time. Can you imagine anything worse? Just thinking about it makes my insides squirm, and trust me, I've been thinking about it a lot. Like . . . Every. Single. Second.

But that horror is six weeks away. Today, I'm supposed to get up on the auditorium stage and pretend to be a famous Californian. That's why I'm currently wearing a costume in the car as Mom drives me to school. Later today, I'll march onto the stage with the rest of my class and stand frozen until the spotlight (a gigantic flashlight wielded by my teacher) hits me. When it does, that's my signal to perform the speech I wrote and memorized. SOLO, with the WHOLE SCHOOL WATCHING.

Everyone in my grade had to pick someone and participate. I chose Grandma Prisbrey, an old lady who built a village out of recycled garbage in the seventies before upcycling was cool, so I figured no one would care enough about my Californian to *really* pay attention to me. (If you've ever sat crisscross applesauce through a school presentation, you know how much mind wandering happens during the boring parts. My goal is to be so mind-numbingly dull that I'm practically invisible.)

My costume is a baggy sweater, old jeans, and a gray wig. Not exactly an attention grabber. Grandma Prisbrey's actually pretty cool once you read about her, but I know I won't get the same *ooh*s and *aah*s and head-snapping attention as Addie Lucas. She chose Mrs. Fields and got special permission to pass out homemade chocolate chip cookies.

Mom turns into the school driveway and queues up behind the long row of cars. As Mom and I inch along in the car line, I rethink my original plan to survive this awful day. I thought I could handle it if I picked someone boring and forgettable (cue Grandma Prisbrey). Now I think I shouldn't even go. My stomach has been hurting since we left the house, and I am practically positive I have a fever.

"I don't feel so well." I let my voice sound groggy and weak.

Mom gives me the look of suspicion. We both have hazel eyes, but hers are lighter than mine because she's older and her pigmentation is flaking away. (In very rare cases, this causes blindness. Mom assures me this is not happening to her. I hope she's right.) "You were fine five minutes ago."

"I wasn't. I didn't mention it because today is a big day. But I think I have a fever."

Mom puts her hand on my forehead. "Definitely not a fever."

I imagine standing onstage while everyone stares at me, and my stomach rolls. "I feel queasy."

Mom hits the breaks as the car in front of her stops to unload. It's a minivan with a billion kids of different ages. My school, Bayside Academy, is of the K–8 variety, so siblings get stuck together for years.

Mom uses the downtime to pull her brown hair into a ponytail and slap sunscreen on her arms. She's a landscape designer. Mostly, she works from home, but sometimes she has to go to client sites. Today is one of those days, and she can't be late. She stressed this several times before we left the house this morning. "You're just nervous, honey. Once you get inside, you'll be fine."

I give her the look of betrayal. Moms are supposed to *want* to care for their sick children.

Mom tries to reason my fear away. "It's simply your cortisol levels run awry. Your fight-or-flight hormones going haywire. Your anxiety making you think you feel sick."

I don't *think* I feel sick. I *do* feel sick.

"You spent a lot of time on that speech and practiced for days and days. It's so good! You're going to be amazing!" Mom uses her cheerleader voice, but her opinion doesn't count. She's my mom. She has to say stuff like that to me.

We somehow manage to creep to the front of the car line in record time, and I start to panic. I really can't go through with this Famous Californian presentation business.

Principal Huxx is overseeing the car line, making sure drop-offs happen quickly and orderly. She used to run a tech company before she decided she needed a profession with meaning, so she likes her school to run extra efficiently. She pulls open the car door with her no-nonsense attitude, and Mom is visibly relieved. She has backup now.

I try to catch Mom's eyes. I need her to save me, but she's ignoring me. It's a game she and I play on rough days. She pretends not to notice my distress. I do my best to show her my anguish (often by holding my stomach and moaning a little). Sometimes she wins. Sometimes I do.

Principal Huxx starts hauling my stuff out of the car, making my odds of victory slim. I'm not a fan of Principal Huxx.

I shouldn't have waited until we were already on the way to school to tell Mom I wasn't feeling well. I should've told her at breakfast. It would have given me more time to convince her that my stomach really does hurt.

Principal Huxx reaches for my wig, but I don't let her have it, which I can tell bothers her. My reluctance to get out of the car is slowing down drop-off. My backpack is already sitting on the curb, waiting for me to collect it. "Prepared for your presentation?"

I try to catch Mom's eyes one last time before I leave the safety of the car, but she's doing a frozen, straight-ahead stare to avoid my gaze while also answering Principal Huxx for me. "She's Grandma Prisbrey. She's been practicing her speech for days. She's going to be great!"

"I look forward to seeing Marvel live up to her potential," Principal Huxx says, and my stomach flippity-flops with the pressure. Now I have to give my speech *and* impress her.

A car behind us honks. The car line is for quick drop-offs. The honk is a friendly one, but the message is clear—move it or lose it.

"Coming?" Principal Huxx asks me in a way that's definitely not a question.

I step onto the curb next to my backpack.

She slams the car door and waves my mom forward.

Finally, Mom looks at me through the rolled-up window. She gives me her biggest smile and two thumbs-ups. Then she speeds away, abandoning me to my doom.

BLANK SLATE

My classroom buzzes with excitement about the presentations. Honestly, I don't get these kids. It's like they don't even see the potential problems. Anything could happen. We could get a bad grade, forget our speeches, blush too much, sweat uncontrollably, get laughed at, fall off the stage, or do some other terrible thing that is yet unknown.

I try to deep breathe the panic away. It doesn't work. I keep getting big whiffs of Addie's chocolate chip cookies, which bring me back to my impending doom.

Addie walks around with a tray, offering homemade baked goods to everyone. She really shouldn't do that. She might run out before the presentations even start, but she looks blissful in her white dress and red apron. I wish I could be like her—relaxed and excited. I don't like being the class worrywart. It's just who I am. Taking my worries away would be like scrubbing the freckles off Addie's face. It can't be done.

Before Addie has a chance to offer me a cookie, our teacher, Ms. Day, makes us line up at the classroom door. From this point, it's just one long march to the stage.

I'm really not feeling good now. It's like a thousand tiny pins are jabbing at my insides. I want to ask my teacher if I can go to the office to call my mom, but I'm trapped between Theo (posing as Steven Spielberg) and Jamie (dressed up as Chet Baker, some dude who played the trumpet), and the line moves me along like a conveyor belt that doesn't stop until we're standing in the curtain wings of the auditorium stage.

I feel hot and sick, but no one seems to notice. That's the thing about anxiety. It happens in the head, and no one sees it. Sometimes I wish I had a broken arm or something. At least then people could see what's wrong with me. They might even sign my cast or ask me how I'm feeling.

Ms. Day walks down the line checking our placement, and my spirits rise. As soon as she gets to me, I'll tell her I'm sick and need to leave. I fixate on Ms. Day like a cat tracking a mouse. She's close, so I'm mere seconds away from rescue.

While my head is turned toward her, Jamie (the most

obnoxious kid at Bayside) blows his trumpet in my ear.

I nearly jump out of my skin. I whip my head around and give him a death glare.

He falls over laughing.

I really don't like that kid.

I turn back toward Ms. Day. She's already three kids down the line. Jamie's little joke made me miss her, and I'll never forgive him for it.

I try to get Ms. Day's attention by frantically waving my arms over my head, but she doesn't see me. No one notices me at all, and before I can get out of there, the stage lights flicker.

"Showtime, people! This is it!" Ms. Day shouts like we should be excited.

Only, I'm not. I'm terrified—knee-knocking, heart-pounding fear. But I can't escape. I have no choice but to suck it up and power through. Mom's right. I've been practicing for weeks. I know my speech. I'll just say it quickly, and it will be over. It's thirty tiny seconds—not even a full minute. *I can do it. I can do it. I can do it.* I shake my hands to release the jitters.

Addie is leading the line. She moves forward.

The rest of us follow, moving ahead with baby steps like a slow-motion conga line.

As we shuffle past Ms. Day, she says, "Don't forget to smile for the camera."

What? Camera? I tap Theo (one of the nicest kids at Bayside) on the shoulder as our line creeps along. "What does Ms. Day mean by *camera*?"

He looks at me like I'm from Mars. "They're going to record our speeches so we can review them together in class. She told us yesterday. Don't you remember?"

I shake my head like a gyroscope. I definitely do not remember that. Most likely, I was in the office with a stomachache when my teacher dropped that particular bomb. "I thought they only recorded the play?"

Theo shrugs and moves forward with the line. "Some parent volunteered to do it, I guess."

I gape at him and stop moving. Kids pile up behind me.

I'm not going out there. Cameras were never part of the deal.

Jamie pokes me in the back. "Move."

"No." I'm not letting them record me making a fool out of myself.

As the front of the line continues to march onto the stage, a space begins to open up in front of me, but I don't want to go forward. I want to go back. I turn around and try to go in the other direction. I'm a salmon swimming downstream while the rest of the school is swimming up.

I plow into Jamie.

He pushes me off him. "Knock it off, Marvel."

When did Jamie get so big? He's a brick wall blocking my escape. "Stop it. Let me through."

"I can't! There're too many people behind me. Just walk, weirdo." Instead of getting out of the way, he moves forward, pushing me toward the stage like a bulldozer.

This kid has a serious problem. He needs to let me through. "Stop it, Jamie. Get out of my way," I hiss at him.

"Shut up, Marvel," he hisses back. He sounds furious but the weird thing is he's smiling. "Turn around, you freak."

I turn . . . and that's when I see them—hundreds upon hundreds of beady kid eyes staring right at me.

Holy moly. I'm onstage.

The whole school is there. The front rows are filled with the little kids, the kindergartners and the lower school students—first through fifth grade. The back rows are filled with the upper school kids and the scariest of the bunch—the eighth graders.

Around the perimeter of the room, the teachers stand watch like guards. I mean, it's almost as if they expect someone up on stage to make a break for it, which isn't entirely bananas because I just tried to run.

I glance over at Jamie and glare. Me being out here is all his fault.

He ignores me.

One by one, kids head to the microphone to give their speeches.

In the center of the aisle, there's a camera so big someone must have stolen it from a movie set. It's obviously recording because there's a red light on top of it that I can't stop staring at.

Ms. Day stands next to the giant camera with her flashlight. Every thirty seconds, she turns it on and off as each new kid walks up to the mic to recite their speech.

I cannot believe this is happening.

I don't hear what anyone else says because I'm too busy wiping my sweaty palms on my jeans and trying to slow my heart down.

I know I can't do it. I can't say my speech. No way, no how. I mean, jumping out of a plane would be easier, and I would never, ever do that, so this speech is definitely not going to happen.

I can't even stand on the stage for one more second, but there's no escape. I'm trapped.

I'm so freaked out I don't hear anything that is happening around me. I don't even realize Theo has given his speech and come back to his place in line until Jamie pokes me in the side. "You're next."

I turn toward him with bulging eyes. "What?"

"Go," he says through gritted teeth, and pushes me.

For crying out loud, what does that kid have against me? I stumble toward the microphone.

Ms. Day flashes the light at me.

I try to speak.

I really do. Except I can't get any words to come out. My mouth is a desert, so dry it won't work, but it doesn't matter because I can't remember words anyway.

I mean, no words at all. I'm a blank slate. The universe before the big bang.

Ms. Day turns the flashlight off and back on again as if that's the problem.

She wants me to talk, but I can't. I don't know how.

My heart takes off like a speed racer, and I start to breathe in short, rapid gulps.

The quicker I breathe, the more air I need, but I can't seem to get enough.

That unknown bad thing I was worried about is happening, and I try to get myself under control so I can make it stop and get off this stage.

I tell myself to take deep, slow breaths, but I'm a runaway cable car hurtling downhill.

My head begins to feel woozy.

My ears start to ring.

My hands go numb.

My legs turn to lead.

And then my entire body freezes. Ceases to work. Refuses to function.

I can't move.

I can't speak.
Not.
One.
Single.
Word.

FROZEN

I stand onstage frozen like a block of arctic ice, petrified into a human statue by uncontrollable full-body panic. The only thing that functions right is my heart, which beats so hard, so fast, and so loud that I'm surprised the microphone doesn't pick up the rapid thumping.

A buzzing sound fills the room as a trillion kids begin to talk about me.

Ms. Day turns the flashlight off and on again, demanding that I speak, but I can't.

I start to sweat. It pools into my palms and on my forehead. A drop slides down my face, and there's no way it's going to go unnoticed by the hundreds of judgmental kids gawking at me and recording me with their contraband cell phones.

I breathe faster and the microphone echoes my panicked puffs around the auditorium.

It's been at least fifteen seconds since I approached the microphone. As I stand there frozen, I start to count the accumulating seconds in my head ... twenty ... twenty-five ... thirty ... I should be done with my speech, but instead of wrapping up, I'm a slow-motion catastrophe unfolding before my very own eyes. I know I'm going to end up on YouTube or turned into a meme.

Thirty-five seconds zooms by, but it feels like hours.

The buzzing turns to laughter. Like a sonic wave, it starts from the back of the auditorium with the eighth graders and washes forward over the other grades until it overtakes everyone—even the little kids in front.

From the very back row of seats some kid shouts, "Get her off the stage!"

This starts a chorus of chants, and soon more kids are yelling, "Get her off the stage!" Even a couple of the little ones in the front row join in, thinking it's some kind of funny game.

Teachers call for quiet, but no one is listening. It's a full-scale riot.

I agree with them. I want to get off the stage as fast as possible, but I can't figure out how to move. The only thing that seems to work right is my eyes. I shoot them toward the stage wings, desperate for an escape route.

Instead, I see Principal Huxx striding toward me. As soon as the kids notice her, a hush falls over them. She walks across the stage purposefully and quickly. When she reaches me, she puts her hands on my shoulders and leans into the microphone, "Let's hear it for Marvel McKenna, everyone!"

Oh. My. God. I can't believe she said my first and last name. Up until that moment, I was an unknown sixth grader in an old-lady costume. I mean, of course my name would get around, but as a *rumor*. Not as a *fact*. Thanks to Principal Huxx, my identity has been caught on camera to be replayed over and over again. My name and image will be forever linked with the LOSER who froze onstage in front of the ENTIRE SCHOOL.

Ms. Day is the first person to start pity-clapping. Then the other teachers join her.

"Time to go, Marvel," Principal Huxx says, and uses my shoulders to try to steer me off the stage, but I don't budge. I can't.

Pockets of snickers erupt from the kids despite Principal Huxx's authoritarian presence.

She glares at them and gives me a nudge to prod me into moving.

I stay stuck.

Principal Huxx leans down close to me and says, "Walk,

Marvel." The microphone picks up her words, and they ricochet around the auditorium.

I want to. I really do, but I can't. I stand there, wide-eyed and stock-still.

Everyone loses it. The kids roar with laughter. Even the teachers have trouble holding it together.

Principal Huxx huffs, not even pretending to be in control anymore. She beckons to the PE teacher, who dashes up on stage. When he gets to us, Principal Huxx says, "Help me out here. Get her feet."

The PE teacher grabs my legs, and my upper body tips into Principal Huxx's waiting arms. She's a lot stronger than she looks.

They hoist me up and carry me offstage like a rolled rug. Gales of laughter burst from the audience again, and I might actually die of shame.

As we pass by Addie, she asks, "Is Marvel okay?"

"Just some stage fright," Principal Huxx says.

That's the understatement of the year. This isn't stage fright. This is a complete and total full-system meltdown combined with an out-of-body experience capped off with the most embarrassing moment of all time.

GLOWWORM

Principal Huxx and the PE teacher lug me through the backstage area and out the door. They set me on my feet, and the PE teacher leaves me alone with Principal Huxx.

It's weird, but outside, it's a normal NorCal day—blue skies, white clouds, and bright blooming flowers everywhere. I was kind of expecting to see a massive chasm in the ozone or a black hole implosion because that's exactly what just happened to my world.

I wiggle my fingers and wave my arms, testing them. Then I do a couple of deep knee bends. My body appears to be working again, which is both confounding and a relief.

Principal Huxx watches me with thinly veiled annoyance. I know I exasperate people. I only wish they knew how much I frustrate myself. It's not like I want to be the way I am or want my body to mysteriously stop working.

"All better now, Marvel?" She's not being mean exactly, but she isn't being super nice either, which seems unsympathetic considering what I've just been through.

"Yes," I say, even though I'll never be okay again.

"Good. Follow me," Principal Huxx says.

Despite my quick once-over, I'm utterly stunned when my feet do their normal thing and walk. I thought they were broken. Fascinated by their sudden reliability, I stare down at them as they carry me along.

Principal Huxx escorts me all the way to the office and uses our time together for a teachable moment, which I totally don't need. "Why didn't you let someone know you weren't up for the presentation? You're in sixth grade now. You need to advocate for yourself."

I want to tell her I did tell my mom, and I tried to tell Ms. Day, but no one listened to me. I don't say anything, though. I'm too busy mentally assessing my body, amazed it's working, and questioning if it's going to stay that way or suddenly decide to freeze again.

We get to the main office, and Principal Huxx pauses at the door to inspect me like she's wondering how I got so hopelessly defective. To be honest, I'm wondering the same thing.

Principal Huxx seems to figure out my issue because

she says, "You let your anxiety get the best of you today, and that's not a pattern you want to fall into."

No kidding.

"You've got to take control over your own life. Believe in yourself. Be the master of your destiny." She sounds like she's reading quotes from inspirational posters.

I nod. It's not the first time an adult has wanted to pep-talk me into a different person. It doesn't work. If a pep talk had magic healing powers, don't they think I'd use one on myself? In fact, I literally just tried to do it a few minutes ago while onstage, and the whole school saw how that worked out.

"I suppose you'll want someone to call your mother to pick you up?"

Of course I do. Holy cow! She can't possibly think I'm going back to class to face those people. I should have said my last goodbyes as soon as I got to Bayside before the *incident* happened because I'm NEVER EVER coming back here again. I've been begging Mom to homeschool me for a while now. This is the perfect moment for that transition.

"Marvel, do you want someone to call your mom?"

I must have spaced off. "Yes." A thousand times yes.

"I'll drop you off with Skippy, then."

Skippy is the school nurse. She and I are quite close. Because of my stomachaches, we spend a lot of time together. It will be nice to have a final goodbye with her.

Principal Huxx leaves me with Skippy and goes into her office or to wherever it is she goes. Principal Huxx has a way of being everywhere at once, which is part of the reason she's so scary.

Skippy, on the other hand, isn't scary at all. She's well into her eighties, with rosy cheeks and eyes that twinkle. I'm not kidding.

Someone must have already filled her in on what happened because she seems to have all the details (see what I mean about the way news travels) and gets busy checking me over.

She takes my temperature.

Normal.

Checks my blood pressure.

Normal.

Shines a bright light in my eyes.

Normal.

Tests my reflexes.

Normal.

"Looking good, Marvel." She hands me an ice pack, even though nothing is bruised, and gives me a juice box.

I'm both surprised by her assessment and not. At the moment, I feel physically fine. Emotionally I'm a complete wreck. I didn't imagine what happened to me up there on stage. If this is the start of an ongoing unexplained medical phenomenon related to my anxiety, that's next-level. I might need to see a specialist.

Skippy pats me on the knee. "Rest here until your mom can pick you up."

I nod, relieved to have a place to hide until Mom rescues me and I never have to see any of these people ever again.

To my complete dismay, Mom isn't able to pick me up right away, and I spend the rest of the morning lying around in Skippy's office. It's really boring, and the hours drag by slowly. There's nothing to do except lie on a cot with crinkly paper. With all the idle time, it's impossible not to replay the events of the morning over and over in my head. It's called rumination, and I'm supposed to work on it, but I don't know how to stop my brain from thinking.

By lunchtime, I've ruminated so much that I burn myself out like an exploding star. I'm still utterly humiliated, but I don't feel the total-body panic like I did before. With time to think about other things, I start to wish I hadn't gotten freaked about my Famous Californian presentation. I really did work super hard on my speech, and it would have been great if a few kids had learned a little something about Grandma Prisbrey. Since I didn't do my talk, a whole generation of kids is going to think everyone in California is either a gold miner, a director, a musician, or a cookie baker. Without me, there was no one to represent the octogenarians. (That means "old people." Internet research can be very educational.)

When the clock says 2:35, the phone rings and Skippy answers it. I can tell she's talking to my mom by what she says.

"She's fine. I've checked her out and have been observing her all day. I'm not concerned." Skippy pauses and nods. "She's more embarrassed than anything. Stage fright happens. I have to admit, her reaction was rather dramatic." There's a long break in Skippy's end of the conversation, and for a second, a flicker of unease turns her lips down. "How far is the walk?" When she hears the answer, she perks up, all traces of apprehension gone. "Oh, that close? She'll be fine. Not to worry. I'll tell her to call you when she gets home."

I don't like what I'm hearing.

Skippy hangs up the phone. "It took your mom a while to get out of her meeting, and then she got stuck in traffic on her way here. There was an accident on the Bay Bridge."

My stomach drops like I'm on an elevator. I immediately imagine the worst.

Skippy holds up a hand. "Nothing to worry about, dear. Your mom is fine, but she's not going to make it here in time to drive you home before the final bell."

I'm shocked by this news. Mom *always* picks me up. "She's not coming?"

Skippy's face is kindness sprinkled with understanding. "She's been doing her best to get to you all day. She's beating herself up pretty hard, but sometimes life gives us more roadblocks than freeway."

Skippy pats my arm, and I feel a bunch of ways at once—humiliated, ashamed, frustrated, and sad. Really, really tired of being me. The whole day slams into me, and I start to feel tears, but I don't let them come. As quickly as I can, I stuff it all back down. As far down as it will go. I only work one way. I can't think too hard about the kind of kid I am or the kind of kid I should be—the type who aces presentations and doesn't need her mom to pick her up all the time. If I do, it hurts. Way too much.

Skippy watches me. I think she's making sure I'm not going to cry. Skippy seems to decide I won't turn into a faucet because she says, "You'll have to walk home. Your mom said it was very close and your older brother will be there waiting for you."

I don't like walking home. It's true that I only live five minutes away from Bayside. Really. I can practically see it from my house. It's just I don't like walking across the sports field. There are always eighth graders hanging out in groups, goofing around, and texting. It's intimidating.

It's why I make my mom drive me even though it's a waste of natural resources. Life is full of competing choices. It's very stressful.

Skippy calls up to my classroom and asks Ms. Day to send down my stuff.

Addie brings my backpack and a cookie. I'm glad it's her. Addie is the one person who might be my friend. I'm not sure, though. I like Addie, but because of my stomachaches, I'm not always in class or at lunch when the stuff that makes people friends happens, so our status is unclear.

"I saved you one." Addie hands me the cookie. "Sorry you . . ."

She doesn't know what to say, so my mind fills in the blanks for her—freaked out, made a fool out of myself, went bananas, completely lost it.

"Missed everything," Addie says.

"Thanks." It was nice of Addie to bring me the cookie.

"How'd the rest of the presentations go?" I hope she says it was awful. I don't wish bad things for Addie or anyone else, but I'm starting to think I missed out.

"Awesome!" Addie sounds like she just got home from the moon. "Everyone loved the cookies. And Ms. Day told me I was a born orator. That means 'speaker,' which is totally great because that's the whole point of this semester, isn't it? To learn public speaking skills?" She's shining from the inside out, and I wonder if Addie is part glowworm.

"Yep. Yes, it is," I say, knowing my failure of sixth grade is imminent, which is one more reason to homeschool. I mean, if this whole semester is about public speaking, I think I've proven it's not going to go well for me. If Addie is part glowworm, then I'm 100 percent earthworm, unremarkable and disappointing.

Addie leaves, and I stuff my wig into my backpack.

Now that all my limbs and extremities are in perfect working order, I can't help wishing someone had heard my Grandma Prisbrey speech and called me a great orator.

Another day down. Another opportunity lost.

I guess I better get used to disappointment because apparently this is my new normal. Yippee for me. I've aced the one thing no one aspires to ever—failure. I wonder if Principal Huxx has a pep talk for that.

The bell rings, and I head home.

SOULMATES

I don't know what the sports field looks like to other people, but to me, it's a big, yawning sea of unknown between my school and my house. Every time I get to it, I start to stress. Too much can go wrong. I mean, nothing ever has, but stuff can. And now I freak out and freeze up, so what if that happens on my way home? Would anyone even call my parents if I'm stuck in the middle of the field immobile like a statue? How would they know my mom's phone number? Maybe I need a medical ID bracelet that says, *This is Marvel McKenna. If found, she is not stone, but a real girl with a horrible problem. Please call Anne McKenna 455-555-7555.*

Though, I suppose I don't need to worry too much because I'm never going to school again, so this is basically the last time I'll have to endure this walk.

I take a few deep breaths to fortify myself as I start to pass the scariest part of the field—the baseball diamond. I don't like it because there are dugouts where kids can hide from the alert eyes of adults and a border of thick bushes where raccoons nest because of all the old food scraps left behind after games.

What I hate about it the most is that it's too far from school to go to the office for help and too far from home for my mom to rescue me.

It's no-man's-land.

And that's exactly where I am when I see them—a group of eighth graders standing in a circle by one of the dugouts.

Here's the thing about eighth graders. They're really big. Their growth spurts start to happen at the end of seventh grade, and all summer they grow like mutant soybeans, so that's one thing. The other thing is they're giddy with power. They rule the school, and it goes straight to their heads. Forget the fact that in a few short months they'll be at the bottom of the social ladder again. They don't even think about it. It's like they've never heard of karma. I have an older brother, so I know this for a fact. Everyone sorts themselves out again in high school, but for that one year, beware.

That's why, when I see them, I immediately start to

alter my course to put as much distance between them and me as I can. Walking near that pack of kids would be like diving into shark-infested waters without a cage. Not smart. Especially after the spectacle I made of myself onstage. My frozen freak-out might as well have been a public service announcement for all the bullies at Bayside. *Hey, folks, need to feel better about yourself? Need someone weak and pathetic to pick on? Look no further than Marvel McKenna. She's here to help.*

Only something in the way they're laughing makes me stop and look.

It's a laugh with a mean edge. A sound I know well. I just heard it onstage, and it wasn't the first time. You can't be me—bundle-of-nerves me—and not know what bullying sounds like. I'm just weird enough that sometimes kids (and even grown-ups) want to tease my anxiety out of me. Like that ever works.

Seven kids stand in a tight circle. From my position, I can't see what's in the middle, but I know they have something in there. Nearby is a trash can on its side and garbage strewn all over the place.

A BIG part of me (almost all of me) wants to keep walking. Get out of no-man's-land to one of my safe zones, but I'm transfixed.

I wish I had a cell phone. I've been telling my mom I need one for situations just like this, but she never budges.

If I had one, I could call her or my big brother or, even better, Principal Huxx. She scares everyone. Obviously, I wouldn't use my real name. I'd leave an anonymous tip.

Without a chance of pending rescue, I know I should move along, let whatever is happening be, but then a girl pushes out from the circle, wiping tears from her eyes. As she passes me, she mumbles, "Jerks. That poor thing. They're so mean."

In the space she's left, I see a tuft of black-and-white fur about the size of a schnauzer but not exactly the right shape or color for a dog. I step closer to get a better look.

It's a . . . baby goat.

Which makes no sense. I don't live in the country. I live in a regular suburb in the shadow of San Francisco. People keep dogs and cats for pets, not farm animals, but the creature in the circle is definitely a goat.

She's mostly white with a mask of black around her eyes and three of her feet, making her look like she's wearing socks but forgot to put one on, which is really adorable. Though, the cutest thing about her is her droopy black ears. When she moves, they flop around the sweetest face I've ever seen. She's like a living, breathing stuffed animal.

She makes a baby bleating noise, and I think I'm in love.

"Watch this," a boy who looks vaguely familiar says. Then, out of nowhere, he claps his hands really loud and screams, "Boo!"

I practically jump out of my skin, but that's nothing compared with what happens to the tuft of fur. She freezes up. Just like I did onstage, but instead of remaining upright, she tumbles onto her side and stays there.

Most of the kids laugh like it's the funniest thing they've ever seen. She's only down a few seconds before she scrambles to her feet again, which renews the kids' laughter.

They think it's funny to purposely frighten her, but it's cruel. Bile rises in my throat. I feel that goat's helplessness and fear like it's my own.

My whole life, I've never felt brave, and I don't feel one ounce of courage now, but after the day I've had, I know I can't let them scare that goat again, and they're going to do it.

Suddenly, those emotions I pushed way down deep pop back up to the surface like ghost ships and whack-a-moles. All at once, I'm sad, embarrassed, ashamed, mad, and tired. Really, really tired of being me—the kid who lets every opportunity blow by her, the dud who watches from the sidelines as the world races past, the scaredy-cat who would walk away and let an innocent creature suffer. Before I even understand what's happening, all those clanging emotions make something inside me wake up, and for once in my life, I'm not thinking. I'm doing.

I run into the circle and throw my arms around the goat's neck.

She's cute as a button, with little nubs for horns and wiry fur that pokes the back of my arms. She doesn't seem to mind my arms around her and pushes her head into my cheek before nibbling at the collar of my T-shirt.

The kids are silent and still. Apparently, my sudden appearance has stunned them.

I'm pretty stunned myself, and I look around the circle, not sure what to do next. There are six kids as tall as beanstalks and just one of me—anxious, cowardly me.

But as I stare at those middle school faces, unsure of what to do, the little goat gnaws at my T-shirt, her mouth tickling my chin, and the defenseless sweetness of her makes me feel the wrongness of injustice in a way I never have before. The strong should *never* pick on the weak.

Something deep inside me starts to burn, and I'm fuming. I think my blood is actually starting to boil, and just then, when I'm angrier than I have ever been in my entire life, I recognize one of the middle schoolers. It's Jamie. The trumpet-blaring, escape-route-blocking, most obnoxious kid in my grade. At first, I didn't realize it was him because he's hanging out with a bunch of older kids I don't know and has somehow gotten so big this year that he blended right in with them.

But seeing Jamie there makes me even madder, and before I know it, I'm yelling nonsense. "Run! Principal Huxx is coming. Principal Huxx is coming." I have no idea where this lie comes from, and I'm awed by how believable I sound because my hands are shaking like leaves and my heart is beating so fast I think I might freeze up again. But for the first time in my life, none of my symptoms are happening because of nerves. It's righteous fury, and it's powerful.

It's also effective. Most of the kids take off like the guilty.

The only ones who stay behind are Jamie and an older boy who looks so similar to him it must be his brother.

Unfortunately, Jamie swings his trumpet case and laughs, not worried in the slightest. "Good one, Marvel."

Jamie's brother elbows him in the side. "Dude, is that the girl that totally freaked out onstage this morning?"

"Yep, Matt. That's her." Jamie smirks.

"Duuuude, that was sick! Especially when Principal Huxx had to drag her off the stage. Funniest thing to happen since I've been at Bayside." He points at me as if I'm not actually a person, but a punch line.

I stroke between the goat's horns. She leans into me, pressing her side into mine as if she's trying to hide from the boys. I don't blame her. I feel my adrenaline draining out of me and my surge of bravery along with it. I want to hide too, but I have to stay with the goat. I can't leave her alone with these two.

"Oh, oh, dude. Show her what happens to the goat when you scare it," Matt says.

I pull the goat closer to me. "No. Don't. I already saw it. You can't do it again."

Matt balks. "Why not? It's totally funny."

"I don't think she likes it." I mean, it doesn't take a rocket scientist to figure out that no one, not even a goat, would enjoy freezing up and toppling over.

"We're not hurting the stupid thing. It's a fainting goat, blockhead. That's what it's supposed to do," Jamie says.

"How do you know that?"

"Duh. YouTube. Funny pet videos," Jamie says like I'm brainless. "It's the best. Look, Matt's been recording her."

Matt starts to show me his videos. I can't decide if these two are bullies or oafs.

"We're going to edit it together into a hilarious montage," Jamie offers, as if that makes it okay, which it doesn't. It makes it so much worse.

"You can't. It's mean to scare her on purpose." I spend way too much time feeling afraid to think it's a laughing matter and I'm definitely not letting them record her anymore.

"It doesn't hurt it," Matt says.

"Her," I correct. "She's a living creature, not an it."

"*It* could be a boy."

I raise my eyebrows at him. Yep, they're oafs.

"Well, it doesn't hurt *her*," Matt says.

"Maybe not physically, but you don't know how she feels inside." But I do. If anyone understands fear, it's me. I pull her face toward me protectively. She nips my ear before pulling away to eat garbage, but I stay where I am, kneeling on the ground near her in case she needs me.

"It's a goat," Matt says, exasperated.

"*She's,*" I correct again. "Besides, is she even yours?" I'm positive Jamie's family does not own a goat.

"No, we found her eating garbage but . . ."

I pull an old food wrapper from her mouth. "Then you have no right harassing her."

"Yeah, so what are you going to do about it?" Matt's eyes narrow, and his mean streak shows. Yep, he's a bully.

My heart starts to beat fast again, and my palms start to sweat. I turn my head toward my house and try to calculate if, carrying the goat, I can outrun Jamie and his brother. Not likely.

I pull out the only threat I have. "If you don't leave her alone, I'll run back to Bayside and really get Principal Huxx."

Matt turns to his brother. "She wouldn't, would she?"

"Probably," Jamie says. "She's a total jerk tattletale."

I try not to move a muscle. I think my threat might have

actually worked, but I don't want to jinx it.

To my complete surprise, the boys begin to leave.

I'm amazed it works. I start to feel rather proud of myself.

Then the goat butts me with her head. The force of it is unbelievably hard for a baby, and I lose my balance. I topple over dramatically, arms and legs thrashing like one of those ridiculous wind-sock guys.

Matt pulls out his phone and starts recording me.

Jamie roars with laughter and yells, "GET HER OFF THE STAGE!"

The poor little goat freezes up and tumbles over, landing on her side next to me.

"They're perfect for each other," Jamie says, laughing his head off.

Matt high-fives his brother. "Score! Let's get out of here and leave the dippy kid with her defective goat. We've got a video montage to edit."

Great, more videos of me making a fool out of myself. As they walk away and leave me alone with the goat, I decide to worry about it later because I know I will.

We both scramble up. The goat starts munching on garbage, and I brush myself off. Jamie's right.

We're perfect for each other.

HOMECOMING

I inspect my new friend.

She's wearing a frayed, battered collar with a tarnished tag that says one word—*Butter*, which must be her name—but there aren't any other details. No phone number. No address. Nothing.

Despite the lack of information, there's no doubt in my mind Butter has an owner. Otherwise, she wouldn't have that collar. Although, one look at her condition, and it's clear the person responsible for her doesn't deserve her. Butter's fur is matted with mud, she stinks like garbage, and she's been left to fend for herself for who knows how long. Between bored middle schoolers, scavenging raccoons, and a trash diet, it's a miracle she's still alive. This little goat needs someone to protect her.

I run my hands over her back and legs, making sure she doesn't have any cuts or alarming injuries. (I realize I'm not a vet, but my anxiety makes me hyperaware of medical problems that could happen—broken bones, festering sores, embedded splinters—so in a way, I'm the next best thing.)

She cranes her neck around and watches me with eyes the color of Mom's hydrangeas. The unusual hue and the emotion shock me. I didn't know goats could have pale blue eyes or the ability to pierce a human's heart. As she looks at me, I get the impression she's trying to tell me how scared and lonely she's been.

"You're okay now. I got you," I say, reassuringly stroking the side of her face. She leans her head into my palm, and I feel the weight of her trust.

I continue to caress her cheek while I finish my examination, and she waits patiently.

Despite being dirty and smelly, she seems healthy. While she definitely needs a bath, she's still the cutest creature I've ever seen. Her spotted fur is slightly puffy like a baby chick's, and one of her knobby knees has a black patch.

There's a dent on the top of her head between her horns, and when I scratch there, her fluffy white tail wags like a dog's. "You like that, do you?"

She tilts her head toward me, and I swear, she gazes at me as if she wants to speak.

It's not a question of *if* I'm going to take her home, but *how*.

I have three choices: coax her into following me, attach a leash to her collar, or carry her.

As an experiment, I take a couple steps away. "Butter. Butter, come on," I say, my voice three octaves higher than normal.

She stares at me.

I pat my knees. "Come on, girl, let's go home."

She blinks and cocks her head to the side.

Well . . . that's not going to work.

I rummage around my backpack for something to use as a leash, but since I'm not in the habit of carrying around rope, I don't find anything. So, option number three is the winner.

I scoop Butter up.

At first, it's awkward trying to get her situated, but once I do, her little goat legs cross in the front, and she rests her head into the crook of my neck.

And off we go.

We're getting close to home when she starts to squirm. "We're almost there," I tell her, and she seems to understand because she calms. I hug her tight to me and pick up my pace.

When we reach my house, I set her down and open the gate.

My house is like something out of a storybook. It literally has a white picket fence. There's also a ginormous garden in the back. It's five times the size of our actual house and is overgrown, but somehow tidy at the same time with all kinds of flowers, herbs, and vegetables planted in rows of containers. It's my mom's pride and joy and the perfect home for a goat.

I know I can't simply plop Butter down and turn her loose in Mom's garden. I value my life too much. I need a solid plan for Butter's housing and care, one that includes persuasive counterpoints for all the objections Mom will throw at me. She's not going to be easily talked into letting me keep Butter.

To form the best argument, I need to become an expert on goat facts fast, and for that, I need the Internet. I carry Butter into the house.

My big brother, Reef, is in the family room. He's got his head down, intensely focused on his cell phone. (Don't even get me started. Reef got a phone when he graduated from elementary school. I have to wait until the end of eighth grade because Mom signed a stupid PTA pledge to keep phones out of the hands of middle schoolers.)

I try to tiptoe by without him noticing. This is not as silly as it sounds. Cell phones mesmerize Reef. Imagine a snake in front of a charmer.

I almost make it to the hallway.

"Hold it," Reef says.

I stop. Unfortunately, my brother is the boss of me when my parents aren't home. Curse birth order.

"What the heck do you have there?" Reef slips his phone into his pocket and comes toward us. He's in the eleventh grade and he's huge. He's all arms and legs and muscles. (He also has a scrawny, fuzzy mustache that he *accidentally* forgets to shave. I'm not allowed to point this out to him, even though SOMEONE needs to tell him. It's like letting him walk around with spinach in his teeth.)

"Reef, meet Butter. Butter, meet Reef." I take one of Butter's legs and wave hello with it.

"Wow. Mom's going to blow her top."

"Maybe not. Look at this face." I hold Butter's muzzle à la proud, cheek-squeezing grandma.

He shakes his head. "She's totally going to lose it. You're lucky Dad isn't here."

"Dad's never here." He's in the navy and is on sea duty. He spends most of his time on a ship that floats around gigantic oceans, which means he can't come home often. He does get leave, but his last deployment has been a long one—almost a year.

"That's not his fault. It's his job." Reef always defends Dad, but he's had more time with him. When Reef was little, Dad had land duty. He went to work during the day and came home at night like a normal father doing a safe, boring job, so he knows him better. The two of them had time to bond. Me, not so much. I feel like I hardly know Dad at all.

"Yeah, yeah. I know." I don't want to argue with Reef about Dad. I hate thinking about Dad because, when I do, all I see is his ship bobbing like a rubber ducky in a raging sea. My version of Dad's world is a mash-up of *Jaws* and every shipwreck scene ever filmed.

I'm scared he might not come home at all or that, when he finally does, he's going to be disappointed in me. Despite my name, I'm not exactly a marvel. I'm a jittery jumble of fears, a coward first class. Dad is *literally* a hero. He's the bravest person I know. We're polar opposites.

Reef snaps to attention and pulls rank. "He's coming back."

"I know. Stand down. I'm not staging a mutiny." If I wasn't holding Butter, I'd salute him just to get his goat (pun totally intended).

Reef's cell phone rings. Suzanna's picture pops up. She's his girlfriend. I like her just fine, but we're supposed to pronounce her name with a slight French accent, which I totally don't understand because she's a boring ol' American teenager and not French at all. No one in her family is French, not even distant relatives. To each their own, I suppose.

"Whatever. It's your funeral." Reef swipes his phone

open and turns on the charm. Maybe Suzanna can get him to get rid of that pathetic mustache.

I take Butter into my room and set her on my bed so I can google. My plan for convincing Mom is to create a pros-and-cons list heavy on the pros.

I pull up some pertinent facts and make a list:

Officially, Butter is called a myotonic goat.
Myotonic goats have a genetic disorder called
   myotonia congenita.
Myotonia congenita makes their muscles suddenly
   tighten when something scares them.

The Internet says fainting doesn't hurt them, but as someone who has spent their whole life being afraid of everything and feeling stressed out, it seems unbearable to me. If I fainted every time something frightened me, I'd fall over constantly. That's why I need to be the person to watch over Butter. No one can relate to her the way I can.

I add a few more items to my list:

They are smaller than normal goats.
There are also miniature versions.

She could be a purse goat. Mom would like that. I glance over at Butter to see if I can determine her size.

She's eating my bedspread.

I put her on the floor.

She's about the size of a Lab puppy and already too big to stuff into a purse, but I triple-underline *miniature versions*, anyway. I think that would appeal to Mom.

I google some more important information on housing and food. Butter needs an enclosure, hay, and lots of water, so not too costly to care for. I put an asterisk by *hay*, and at the bottom of the page, I jot down *$200*, my savings account balance, to show Mom I'm willing to pay for Butter's upkeep with my own money. Mom's a fan of ingenuity.

I discover more neat things about goats. They can be trained like dogs (handy), and they communicate with people by making eye contact. (I knew it!) I add these details to my pros column.

I also discover a negative. Goats are foragers. This means they eat everything in sight. I do NOT add this to my list.

I turn to Butter.

She's chewing on my math book as if to prove how good she is at foraging.

I groan and wrestle it from her. My glossy, previously perfect math book is now covered in slime and gnaw marks. A couple of pages are missing edges and one page is completely gone. I scan my room for the remains. Nothing.

I drop to my knees to search under my bed.

Butter joins me, bending her front legs so she can stick her head under the bed next to mine.

I run my hand across the empty space, hoping that my eyes are deceiving me and I'll unearth the missing page so I can repair my book. The only thing I rustle up is a herd of dust bunnies that makes Butter sneeze and scramble back.

My stomach churns as I crawl out from under my bed. The condition of my book when issued to me is inscribed inside the front cover. I flip it open. Written in my math teacher's perfect penmanship is the word *NEW*, as in brand spanking. I'm the first kid to use this book (and the last, apparently). My mind fast-forwards to end-of-the-year book return, when I'll have to account for the condition.

For some reason, I imagine Principal Huxx in judge's robes, all my teachers unhappily crammed into a jury box and the entire school staring at me from the audience as I try to defend myself. My mouth goes dry and I blame my sixth-grade civics unit for the vivid, panic-inducing vision of American justice in action. Whoever said knowledge is power didn't have my anxious brain. My head turns tidbits of information into tiny guerrilla soldiers and stations them around my mind until the perfect moment for attack.

I'm not sure what school will do to me for returning a destroyed math text, but I come up with all kinds of consequences—cafeteria duty, expulsion, summer school. My heart rate kicks up, and I shove the math book under my bed, pushing the object of my torment to the farthest corner, where it can live out the rest of its days with the dust bunnies.

Maybe having Butter in the house is not the best idea.

I pick her up and snuggle my face into her fur. She smells like garbage. "You need to be disinfected."

Butter bleats in agreement, and I vow to give her a bubble bath after dinner.

In the backyard, I pour water into a bowl for her.

Like I said, our garden is huge. There's even a greenhouse for my mom and a work shed for my dad. Dad's a do-it-yourselfer. Unfortunately, he's not always home long enough to finish stuff, so his shed is full of almost-completed projects. In the corner, a puppet theater he started to build for me before he got assigned to sea duty leans against one wall. That was such a long time ago, I barely even remember being into puppets, but the theater will make a good wall for Butter's enclosure.

I drag it into the garden. I remember it being really big, but it was made for nine-year-old me, not twelve-year-old me, so it's totally manageable.

Stepping back, I examine the puppet theater. It's

practically finished. It has a cutout for the stage framed by red curtains. Above the stage, *Marvel's Majestic Theater* is stenciled in pencil, waiting for paint. Other than that, it's done.

My memory of the puppet theater doesn't match what's before me. I thought Dad never even got close to completing it and I was heartbroken. I vaguely remember Mom trying to convince me that she and I could finish it after Dad left. I thought she had gone completely bananas and refused. Now I see that she and I could have easily slapped some paint on it. Wow. I can't believe I missed indulging my geeky puppet obsession all because of missing paint. I might have been a puppet prodigy destined to bring puppeteering to the masses. I spend a single blissful second imagining being a great performer.

Then reality hits me like a jump scare. All the ghastly events of my Famous Californian presentation slam into me—the camera, the speed of my heart, the sweat on my palms, standing frozen onstage, Principal Huxx telling the entire school my name, the kids yelling *Get her off the stage*. Remembering the embarrassing details is like walking through a haunted house, each room getting more and more horrific.

Just thinking about it makes my lungs feel short of air, and I breathe faster, trying to suck more oxygen into my body.

Butter bleats at me.

I look at her.

She's watching me.

I scratch the sides of her muzzle to reassure her. I don't want to infect her with my fear. She's had a really rough day too.

She leans into me.

The weight of her feels solid and warm against my leg.

She gazes up at me, concerned.

"Don't worry. I'm okay." Saying it to Butter somehow makes me pretend it's true. I block all thoughts of school, presentations, cameras, stages, and mocking kids from my mind and focus on Butter—on only her and her needs. Right now, that's an enclosure.

I pick her up and take her into the shed with me.

I let her explore while I rummage around for supplies. I grab a hammer, nails, and some discarded netting.

We go back into the garden, and she watches as I build a home for her.

I use part of our existing fence as the back of her enclosure and the puppet theater as the front. For the sides, I string the netting between them and nail it into place.

It takes longer than I want, but when I'm done, I'm proud of myself.

It's makeshift. The sides are flimsy. It's only landscaping netting, but it should hold Butter until I can figure out a better solution and prove to Mom I'm capable of taking care of her.

I plunk Butter inside to see how she likes it. She wanders around and checks everything out. She makes one complete circle and then bleats at me. She approves.

The timing couldn't be more perfect. I hear a car pull into the driveway. Mom. (I feel like I should hear a drumroll or maybe a funeral dirge.)

I think about the list I made and pray it's enough to convince Mom to let me keep Butter. Not only does Butter need me—the only person in the world who can truly understand what myotonia congenita must be like for her—but I need Butter. I already love her. She's the puzzle piece I didn't know I was missing, and now that I've found her, I can't let her go.

I pet my soulmate one last time and head inside to plead our case.

HOW YOUR GARDEN GROWS

I greet Mom at the front door.

She doesn't look good. Her practical ponytail, typically high and bouncy, has lost its spring. It's like a mangled Slinky. She's grimacing and a tad gray. (I finally understand the term *ashen* that books are always prattling on about.)

If I'm being honest, it's a bit alarming. I pretend not to notice how unhinged she looks. I don't want to embarrass her. I mean, her job as a mom is to keep it together, and she's not exactly at peak performance at the moment.

She embraces me in an epic hug, and I fall into her, the weight of everything that's happened making me feel unhinged myself. Today definitely deserves top spot in my long list of awful days.

She rubs my back soothingly. "I'm sorry I couldn't get here sooner."

"We should probably order a medical ID bracelet for me in case it happens again." My words come out muffled because my head is mushed into Mom's shoulder.

Mom pulls back and holds me at arm's length. "I know today was awful, but that's a *tad* dramatic, don't you think? You got stage fright. It happens. I'm sure no one even noticed." Mom rubs my arms.

Seriously, Mom? I think that's called wishful thinking. "Everyone saw me turn into a block of ice onstage and melt down in front of them. Principal Huxx and the PE teacher had to carry me off the stage."

Mom's eyes pool with sympathy, which makes me feel worse because it confirms I'm defective. "I agree, we've got to get a handle on this. We need to be more proactive about your therapy whether you like it or not."

"What do you mean, *like it or not*?" If it's like it or not, I can already tell it's not.

"For starters, I know you've been resistant to the therapy group Mr. J has been suggesting, but it's time you went." Mr. J is the therapist for our school district. He's at our campus a couple days a week and he's been trying to help me with my anxiety, but I'm a lost cause.

"I'm not resistant to it," I lie. Mom's gone completely bananas if she thinks I'm going to talk about myself and my issues in front of other kids. But I don't want to tell her that. She'll brush my concerns away by saying it's silly to be embarrassed or that the other kids won't judge me. Mom has no idea what kids are really like. How snickering and mean they can act if you're not normal (case in point: Jamie and his brother). If she did, she'd understand why I don't want to confess my deepest, innermost fears to them. The way adults can be so utterly clueless about what it's like to be a kid is baffling.

I say, "I'm resistant to the location. It's a safety hazard."

This is also true. The therapy group in question meets in the school basement. A place with no egress. (*Egress* is a word commonly used in architecture to mean "exit." Landscape designer's daughter here.) No egress means no way out of the basement. If there is an earthquake or a fire during group therapy, I'll be trapped. I don't even have a cell phone to call for help in a situation like that. Maybe I need to put a phone on my list of medical necessities along with an ID bracelet? I mean, the cell phone conversation is one I'd be interested in having.

Mom rolls her eyes. She's got an epic eye roll. I think it comes from raising a teenager. "There's nothing wrong with the location. The school wouldn't put children in danger."

I step away from her. "Really? Because they let me

freeze up. ONSTAGE. In front of EVERYONE. I thought I was dead."

"Marvel, come on, you can't blame that on the school and you weren't in danger."

Maybe I can't blame it on the school, but I can blame it on her. "I told you I didn't feel well and you ignored me. You should've listened!"

"I did. I thought it was nerves," Mom says in defense.

"It *was* nerves. *Freezing nerves*." She needs to understand what she put me through. "If everyone would leave me alone and stop pushing me to do stuff I'm uncomfortable with, I'd be fine!" I don't mean to yell at her, but all my yucky feelings about today are starting to bubble over again.

"Do you want to talk about what happened at school?"

Her question triggers a 4D replay in my mind. I smell Addie's cookies, feel the pins in my stomach, see the camera's red light, hear the kids yelling *Get her off the stage*, and feel the utter shame of making a fool out of myself in front of everyone like I'm swimming in it. I can't tell her about it. I don't want to think about it ever again. Only, my anxiety doesn't work like that. Even when I'm purposely *not* thinking about something, it's there. It's like really annoying background music that never shuts off. I shake my head. "No, I definitely don't want to talk about it. I want to forget it."

"I understand today was horrible, but you can't shut down from the world. If you do, your life will get narrower and narrower. You'll never try anything new or find out what you're capable of." Mom puts her hands on my shoulders and meets my eyes. "You have so much to offer, honey. I wish you could see that."

I know she thinks her confidence in me helps, but it doesn't. It makes me feel worse and reminds me that believing in myself is another thing I'm bad at. "I don't need therapy with other kids. But I agree I need something new, like you said."

"I'm all ears." She's always hopeful something will help. Me too.

I scrunch my face up, doubtful. Mom's lecture stamina is legendary. I'm not sure she's truly done yet.

"For goodness' sake, Marvel. I said I was listening." She looks tired and worn down. Normally, I'd feel bad about that, but having her resistance low for what I'm about to suggest is probably a good thing.

"Okay. If you're *really* listening." Never hurts to heap on a little guilt. "I need a pet."

"A what?"

I'm not sure she understands the word I said, so I spell it out. "I need a P-E-T." I repeat the word spelling bee style. "Pet."

"You want a dog?" She pinches the bridge of her nose

and squeezes. "Marvel, this has been a very difficult day. I've been worried about you for hours . . ."

I interrupt her. "If I had a cell phone, you could've called and checked on me and wouldn't have had to worry for hours." And I would have been able to call for actual help for Butter and me instead of throwing Principal Huxx's name around like it's my weird superpower.

Mom takes a deep breath. "As I was saying, I've been worried about you for hours and your solution is to get a dog?"

"I never said I wanted a dog. I said I wanted a pet," I clarify to keep us on the same page.

"I don't even understand this conversation." Mom goes into the dining room and collapses into a chair.

I follow her. "It's simple. You said I never try anything new and I'm suggesting something new—a pet. See, we both want the same thing."

"Okay, for the sake of argument, and because I'm totally exhausted, you want a pet, but not a dog. What are we talking about here? A hamster?"

"Nope."

Mom sighs, "Goldfish? Because you know they don't live very long."

"Nope." I shake my head.

"Cat?" Mom suggests hesitantly, as if she's been dreading the day I ask for one.

"Something better." I'm tempted to add jazz hands, but I don't want to oversell it.

"Better than a cat? Do you plan on enlightening me?"

"I thought you'd never ask." I pull Mom out of her chair and lead the way to the back door. I'm going to soften Mom up with Butter's adorableness and then pull out my pros-and-cons list to wow her with my logic.

As Mom and I walk through the family room, we pass by Reef. He's lounging on the couch playing video games. As soon as he sees us heading toward the garden, he drops his game controller and hops off the couch. "I can't wait to see this."

"What do you know about it?" Mom asks.

"Nothing. This is all Marvel. But it's going to be awesome." Reef smiles like he's gotten the best gift of his life.

Mom starts to look nervous, so I give Reef my evil-younger-sister glare.

He laughs at me. Big brothers are *really* annoying.

The three of us go into the garden. I can't wait for Mom to meet Butter and see how responsible I've been by making an enclosure for her.

I throw open the door, ready to present Butter to Mom.

Only, there's a problem. A very BIG one. Butter isn't where I left her. Instead, she's roaming the garden like it's her own personal pasture.

"Marvel Madison McKenna! Did you bring a *forager* into my garden?"

How does Mom know about foragers? I planned to keep that information top secret.

"No," I sputter. "I mean yes, but I put her in an enclosure."

"An enclosure she's escaped from!" As a landscape designer, Mom is very invested in growing and nurturing plants. I'm pretty sure Mom likes plants more than people (though I would never say this to her face). I know for a fact she loves our garden more than she loves our house. It's her favorite place in the world . . . and Butter is ravaging it.

Mom stalks toward Butter.

I run after Mom.

Reef hangs back, watching the show.

Butter doesn't notice Mom coming toward her. She's too busy nibbling on a burlap-wrapped sapling. There's been a whole pallet of them sitting in the garden for a few days. They're for Mom's newest landscaping job. None of the trees have any greenery left except the one Butter is happily munching on. Only three leaves remain.

I grab Mom by the arm. "Wait. You have to go slowly. Otherwise, Butter will faint."

She stops in her tracks. Her lips merge into a single line. *"Faint?"*

"I'll explain in a sec." I go to Butter and gently pull her away from the tree.

She's eaten everything except one measly leaf. She jerks away from me, stands on her hind legs, and snags it.

I yank her down.

She burps in my face.

Butter's making an awful first impression. I try to salvage the situation. "Mom, this is Butter. Butter is a fainting goat. I found her. She's homeless. Can I keep her?" The words tumble out of my mouth in a blunt mess and don't sound as eloquent or convincing as I had planned.

Mom's furious. I can tell by the way her eyebrows pull together. "Uh . . . this is an easy one. No. You may not keep the goat."

"Why not?" Instead of laying out a mature, logical argument of pros and cons, I sound like a whiny baby.

Mom looks at Reef. "You should have warned me."

Reef shrugs, completely unfazed. "Hey, this was her thing. I didn't have anything to do with it."

"Later, you and I are going to have a long talk about responsibility," Mom tells him.

He doesn't even seem to care. He's enjoying this way too much.

"You don't understand," I say, pulling Mom's attention away from Reef. "Butter doesn't have anyone else." I want to explain our bond and how much we need each other, but I don't know how to put the tug of love I feel for her into words.

"Marvel, this is absurd. A goat is a farm animal. We don't live on a farm." Mom examines one of her saplings and groans. "These leaves will take weeks to regrow."

I'm relieved. "That's good news! I was afraid she'd killed them."

Mom blasts me with a death glare.

Oops. I offer her an apologetic smile. Then I return to what's important. Mom's plants will survive. Without me, Butter won't. "She needs a home."

"Our house isn't zoned for farm animals, and there's no way we're keeping a goat in our backyard." Mom sounds like she means it.

"But Butter needs *me*. I understand her." I pull Butter's face toward me.

"Yeah, Mom. Marvel *understands* Butter." Reef's not even trying to hide his laughter.

Both Mom and I shoot him evil looks.

Mom spies Butter's tag and points to it. "She has an owner. Otherwise she wouldn't have that."

"There's no information on it, just her name. Besides, her owner is mean and horrible. What kind of person abandons a baby goat? When I found her, she was having to eat out of a trash can and being tormented by kids who thought it was funny to scare her on purpose and record her distress for a video montage. She has a genetic disorder that gives her anxiety. She's like me."

Mom's anger drains away. "That's really sad, but I can't keep a goat in my garden." Mom looks over at the saplings that are now barren sticks. She massages her temples. "She ate my plants. Give her another hour and she'll gobble up everything. There will be nothing left."

I feel the finality of Mom's decision in the air, but I try one more time anyway. "But . . ."

Mom crosses her arms and shakes her head. "We can't, honey. If she were a dog, maybe, but she's not. She's a goat. She doesn't belong here. We'll take her to the humane society. They're better equipped to find her owner or a good home. That's my final answer."

My heart slips all the way down my body and splats onto the ground.

FAMILY DYNAMICS

Mom, Reef, and I stand in the middle of the garden, staring down at Butter.

I bite back tears while Mom looks guilty yet determined and Reef digs a hole in the dirt with his foot, uncomfortable with the impasse.

"What's going on out here?" a deep voice says.

The three of us look toward the house and see my dad standing in the doorway. He's wearing his navy uniform and holding his duffel bag.

Reef doesn't hesitate. He runs to him. "You're home!"

Dad drops his duffel bag and throws his arms around Reef. They do a man hug—all back pats and forearm embraces.

"Oh my goodness, Jack!" Mom's voice cracks, and she runs to him too.

He wraps her in a bear hug.

Mom wipes tears from her eyes and gives him a big smooch. "What are you doing here?"

"Got some unexpected leave," Dad says, and then looks over at me.

I know I should run over to him like Reef and Mom, but I feel weird. Sometimes, after Dad's been gone for a long time, he starts to seem more like a character from a book or movie than a real person. I hear Mom's and Reef's stories of Dad and he sounds amazing—always brave, always strong, sometimes funny. They share all these specific, special details—like the way his Southern accent sounds when he says *sweetheart* or *champ*; that his favorite color is a shade of blue only found in the waters off the Gulf Coast, where Dad grew up; how much he loves cheese grits and insisted Reef try them only to have Reef gag and spit them out, making Mom laugh so hard she doubled over—and I always want to join in these conversations. I want to tell my own stories, but when I search my memories, they're hazy, like something off in the distance.

Then I feel awful because I'm failing him by not remembering right. We're the troops at home. We're supposed to support him by being brave, by being strong, by being okay he's away, by not giving him extra stuff to worry about while he's at sea, and by remembering him perfectly when he's gone so that when he comes home it's not strange.

Only, having Dad suddenly here in real life *is* strange and I'm not sure how to act, so I hang on to Butter like she's the reason I can't greet him properly.

Dad gives Mom and Reef another round of hugs and comes to us instead. "Hey, Marvel. What do you have there?

"This is Butter."

He kneels down and scratches Butter's ears. "I'm surprised Mom let you get a goat." He winks at Mom.

"She didn't." I fill Dad in on Butter and how she came to be in our garden, but I leave a lot of stuff out. I don't tell him about my stage fright or fake-threatening to tell on the kids or any of the stuff that makes me sound like a loser. I can't. Not yet.

"That was brave of you." Dad strokes my hair.

Emotion flickers across Mom's face. It's like sadness and love stirred together. Sometimes, I think Mom feels worse for me than I do.

"I wasn't really." I don't want to take fake credit. He doesn't know the whole story, the defective parts. "I didn't have a choice. I had to help her."

Dad regards me and then nods like we've shared something between us, but I don't know what it is.

Butter bleats and paws Dad's arm.

He smiles and pulls Butter's tag toward him.

"I want to keep her, but Mom says I have to take her to the humane society." I'm ratting Mom out on purpose. I'm angry she's making me give Butter away.

"Is that so?" Dad scratches Butter's head. "She's mighty cute. Did you know my grandpa kept goats on his farm in Louisiana? I loved visiting him."

I stash that tidbit of info in my mind and vow to remember every detail. I'm going to share it the next time Mom and Reef are telling stories after Dad leaves. Because Dad will be gone again as quickly as he arrived.

Dad turns to Mom and shocks me by saying, "We can let her keep the goat until she can find the owner, right? What harm could it do?"

His words spark a glimmer of hope, which Mom immediately blows out. "What *harm*? That goat ate my landscape order and she's been here less than an hour!"

Dad looks from me, to Butter, to Mom, and back again like he wants to make us all happy. "What if she sleeps in the garage for tonight and I build her a proper . . ."

Mom scowls at him.

"*Temporary* enclosure tomorrow," Dad finishes, and my flicker of hope reignites.

Mom and Dad do their mind-meld thing. They don't say a word, but I know they're silently communicating.

I have no idea how they fall back into it so easily after Dad's been away.

I hold my breath, not wanting to move a muscle, afraid I'll jinx the verdict.

Dad must win the argument because Mom relents a little. "Only until she finds the owner. We can't keep a goat as a pet."

"Yes!" I pull Butter toward me and snuggle her in celebration. I'm so happy, I barely notice the trash stench emanating from her fur.

"Don't get attached. She's a guest, not a family member," Mom warns, and then looks at Reef. "You'll help her hang signs and put a notice on Nextdoor."

"Me? Why me?" Reef asks, and I bet he regrets following us into the garden now.

"Because you need to learn responsibility and . . ." Mom pauses, trying to think of more reasons to make Reef help me. "You play too many video games and need something else to do."

"Ugh." Reef rolls his eyes and stomps inside.

Dad laughs. "There's no place like home."

Mom lovingly pats Dad on the shoulder. "Remember, the goat was your idea."

———

The rest of the afternoon goes by quickly. I bathe Butter to get the garbage stink off her and repair her makeshift enclosure. While Dad gets settled, Mom cooks dinner. When it's ready, we decide to eat in the garden so Butter can explore her enclosure with supervision.

We bring all the food to the outdoor table, and it's amazing how full it feels with four people sitting around it instead of three. We linger long after we've eaten, giving Dad, Mom, and Reef time to fill one another in on the last nine months. Dad tells interesting stories about faraway ports. Mom gushes about her newest landscaping job, her biggest one ever. Reef, being good at everything, talks about school, sports, and friends. I listen to them quietly and watch Butter bounce around her pen.

As the hour grows later, it starts to get chilly and the flow of my family's chatter slows. Dad glances at his watch and then me. "Catch me up on your world, Marvel."

Mom, Reef, and Dad look at me expectantly, but I don't want to talk about myself because I don't have any victories to share and the night's been too cozy to ruin with tales of mortifying defeats. "Um . . . well . . ." I stall, trying to think of something, but the only thought in my head is an image of me freezing onstage.

"Was that a raindrop?" Mom asks.

Before we can respond, we all feel them, big round drops dripping from the sky. The night brought the rain along with the chill. We jump up, clearing plates and food before it starts coming down in buckets, and I breathe a sigh of relief. I've been saved from answering Dad's question and gotten a little more time before I have to confess my failures to him.

I bring Butter inside and get her situated in the garage. By the time I'm done, it's time for bed, and despite all the events of the day—my humiliating speech, finding Butter, and Dad's unexpected arrival—I fall asleep quickly.

———

I'm not sure what wakes me up first, the rain or Butter.

Outside, one of our famous Northern California rainstorms rages. Raindrops pound on the roof, and wind shakes the walls. Over it all, I hear Butter bleating. Despite her cozy spot in the garage, she sounds terrified.

I sneak downstairs and quietly open the door leading into the garage.

As soon as Butter sees me, she bounces over.

I scoop her up and carry her to the bed I made for her of old moving blankets. I sit down with her in my lap and sink my fingers into her fur.

Butter snuggles into me and nibbles on my pajama sleeve.

A big gust of wind blows. It rattles the garage door like the whole house is going to fall down. Butter freezes up and goes stiff.

Poor Butter. I stroke her side until she relaxes again. I don't blame her for being scared of the storm. I know exactly how she feels. Personally, I worry about the wind being strong enough to blow the windows apart, sending flying glass and gushing rain into the house. Vivid, I know. My imagination is part of my problem.

She pops up and shakes herself off and then lies down next to me.

I curl myself around her.

Butter pushes her nose into my cheek. It's soft and warm and a bit ticklish.

"You know, Butter, I have anxiety like you," I say, talking to distract her from the loud noises. "Only, I don't think I was born with an anxiety gene. No one else in my family has it and my dad's the bravest person on the planet, so mine isn't genetic. I think mine started from a seed and grew up inside me like a big, giant redwood. Sometimes, I feel like my insides are a whole redwood forest of concerns, one worry pollinating another."

Butter gazes up at me, and I swear she's asking me a question with her aquamarine eyes.

"You're wondering what the seed was? Mr. J, the school therapist, asks me that all the time. I'm not exactly sure, but Mr. J says anxiety is unprocessed feelings coming out sideways." I mimic Mr. J's soothing therapist voice: "'Emotions will get you one way or another, Marvel.'"

Butter bleats at me.

"Shush," I tell her. "You can't make noise or Mom might

change her mind about letting you stay, and I really want to keep you."

Someone clears their throat.

I pick my head up and see Dad. I don't know how long he's been standing there.

He sees me snuggled next to Butter and I wonder if I'm in trouble, but he doesn't say anything. He simply closes the door.

Relieved he's not mad, I lay my head back down, and my eyes start to feel droopy.

After a few minutes, the door opens again. Dad has a blanket and a pillow. He covers me with the blanket and hands me the pillow. "Don't let your mom catch you out here. I think that goat's on borrowed time as it is."

At the thought of losing Butter, sadness coils around my heart like a constrictor and squeezes. I can't let anyone take her away from me, not even Mom. "Don't worry, I won't."

He kisses my forehead and goes to the door.

"Good night," I say, groggy.

"Night, sweetheart. Get some sleep. You have school in the morning." Dad closes the door.

My eyes pop open, and I'm suddenly wide awake. I can't go back there. Not tomorrow. Not ever.

PLANS

I wake up on the garage floor with Butter nibbling on my hair.

"You need a chew toy." I gently push her head away and roll over. I'm exhausted. Dad's parting words about going to school today kept me up fretting and planning how to get out of it.

I finally settled on talking to Mom at breakfast and telling her all the gruesome details of exactly what happened during my presentation. Even though the idea of reliving the whole thing again makes me queasy, once she understands how awful going back to school will be for me, I'll roll out my homeschooling plan.

I even came up with the perfect project—Butter. I can build her a house (math), record and measure her growth (science), study her origins (history), and read books about training (language arts). It's perfect. Mom has to agree.

I kiss Butter on the nose.

She headbutts me.

"Ouch." Cranky. I rub my forehead. She must not be a morning goat or maybe she's hungry. We're still getting to know each other. Another reason why I need to stay home with her instead of going to school. I scoop her up and take her into the house.

Dad's at the stove scrambling eggs. "Morning, you two. How'd you sleep?"

"Okay." I sit down at the table with Butter in my lap. "Where's everyone?"

"Your brother left for school about ten minutes ago, and your mom jetted out of here at the crack of dawn to get to her landscaping project. Something about traffic and reordering plants." His Southern drawl and old-timey slang make him sound like a country singer sometimes. He puts a plate of eggs in front of me.

"She's gone already?" I push my eggs around on my plate. I can't talk Mom into homeschooling me if she isn't here.

Dad watches me play with my eggs. "Don't worry. Dad's on deck. I'll take you to school this morning, and I'll be there at two thirty to pick you up."

I frown and pull Butter closer, trying to focus on the feel of her fur instead of the rolling nausea that wants to overtake me. *No way* I can face school. Everyone is going to laugh at me.

Misinterpreting my expression, he says, "I'll get there before two thirty. I'll be there at two fifteen so I'm ready and waiting as soon as school gets out." He smiles as if he's solved the problem.

"Yeah, okay. Thanks. Um . . ."

"Yes?" Dad pauses and waits for me to say more.

"Yesterday . . ." I want to tell him about my stage fright. The way I couldn't move my legs, couldn't speak, how everyone laughed at me and how embarrassed I am to face the kids at school, only I can't do it. Of course Dad knows I have anxiety. It's not a big secret or anything, but it's one thing to know about it and it's another to live it. Because he's not here most of the time, he doesn't have to drown in the day-to-day details and I don't want to plunge him into it.

He might only be home for a few days. The navy can call him back at any moment. It's happened before. Then he'll be gone again for who knows how long. I don't want to spoil what little time we have by showing him who I really am. How defective. How cowardly. Dad fights in wars. I can't even give a thirty-second speech without sinking into a bottomless ocean of nerves and full-body panic. And if I can't explain why not going back to school matters so much, I can't make a case for homeschooling.

Dad sets another plate down. It has a variety of fruit cut up in tiny pieces. "For Butter's breakfast. I'll find her some goat food while you're at school and work on her enclosure."

"Thanks." I feed Butter a piece of banana.

She gobbles it up and begs for more by pushing her nose into my hand.

Dad laughs, but I can only manage a half-hearted smile at her cuteness. I'm desperate to stay home with them, where things are easy and friendly, instead of going to school.

Dad considers me. "Don't worry about Butter. I'll watch her today."

At the moment, Butter isn't the one I'm worried about. She gets to stay home with Dad.

"Tell you what, I'll finish feeding her and get her secured before we leave. That way you can get ready." Dad holds out his arms for her.

"Okay." I reluctantly hand her over and head to my room to get dressed. On my way, I devise a plan that might help me hide for the six grueling hours of school. As soon as I get there, I'll go straight to Skippy and tell her I feel terrible. If I'm lucky, she'll let me camp out in her office for the day. If not, there's always the bathroom. The one thing I know for sure is that there's NO WAY I'm stepping one single toe into any of my classes.

———

Instead of swinging around through the car line, Dad pulls into the parking lot.

"You aren't dropping me off?" Mom never parks. She stopped in third grade when she realized the walk from the car to my classroom gave me too much time to beg her to take me back home again.

Dad pulls off his baseball cap and rubs a hand over his head, straightening hair that's cropped too short to actually get messy. "Principal Huxx wanted to have a quick chat with you and a parent before school. I told your mom I'd do it. I miss so many of these things."

I practically feel my head exploding. I mean, we're not talking about an open house here or an awards ceremony. I'd be thrilled to have Dad come to those, not that I've ever been to any (there are no awards for Most Anxious and open house is optional, so I opt out), but in theory those are nice events. This is a principal-parent conference. Everyone knows that's not good.

If Dad gets called away tomorrow, the memory of me he'll take with him for however many months he's gone is whatever happens next. After yesterday, let's face it,

Principal Huxx isn't calling us in to celebrate my unique way of handling presentations.

This is not good. Not good at all.

When we get to the office, Ms. Day is waiting for us. I suppose everyone but me got a heads-up about this meeting.

"Good morning, Marvel," Ms. Day says sweetly. She's a first-year teacher, so she's brand-new and not worn out yet, which is nice because she's almost never grumpy.

"Hi, Ms. Day." My school voice is different from my home voice. The one I use at school sounds shakier and kind of shy.

Ms. Day extends her hand to Dad. "You must be Captain McKenna. Your wife mentioned you'd be coming in today. I'm Marvel's homeroom and core teacher. That means I have her for social studies and language arts. I'm also her main point of contact."

Dad pumps her hand vigorously, all warmth and smiles. "I've heard a lot about you."

I glance at him, surprised by his revelation. I haven't mentioned Ms. Day to him once, which means Mom has been talking to him about me. I hope she's only telling him good stuff.

Ms. Day touches my shoulder. "I bet it's nice to have your dad home."

I nod. I am happy he's home, but it makes it harder to

hide the realities of my anxiety from him. When he's at sea, Mom's the only parent at these meetings and I don't need to impress her because she's around me 365 days a year. Our time together isn't limited.

"And you're enjoying the time off?" Ms. Day asks Dad.

"Yes, ma'am. It's great to have some time at home. These rascals grow like weeds when I'm at sea." He nudges me and chuckles, like we're at a backyard barbecue. I'm not sure he understands the gravity of our situation.

"I bet they do," Ms. Day says. I can tell she likes Dad. He's not in uniform, but the way he stands and acts shouts serviceman and military hero. I'd be so proud to introduce him to her if the reasons for this meeting were different.

"Why don't you both follow me to the conference room." Ms. Day ushers us down a hallway and into a small room with a table too large for the tight space. "Principal Huxx will join us momentarily."

Dad and I squeeze around the table and sit on the side farthest away from the door. I immediately start to feel trapped and claustrophobic. Dad seems relaxed and not bothered at all. I suppose all his time on ships has trained him to be comfortable in close quarters.

Ms. Day positions herself across from us and clasps her hands in front of her expectantly.

As soon as we're settled, Principal Huxx strides into the room carrying a thick file and sits next to Ms. Day.

Facing off with them makes my stomach feel hollow, and I bite my bottom lip, dreading what Principal Huxx might say.

"Glad you could join us today, Captain McKenna," Principal Huxx says formally, and flips open the overflowing file.

Dad nods and matches her tone as if he's finally starting to realize the true nature of this meeting. "Nice to see you again, Principal."

Principal Huxx directs her ceremonial niceties toward me. "Recovered from your stage fright?"

I flinch and cut my eyes to Dad to check his expression. He's facing forward, so only his profile is visible, but his jaw seems tighter than before and I wonder if that tension is in reaction to learning I've developed yet another anxiety to add to the million others I already have or Principal Huxx's curt tone.

"Yes," I lie because she's the last person on the planet I want to talk to about it, especially with Dad sitting right there.

"Glad to hear it," Principal Huxx says, all business. "Marvel, your teachers and I had a chance to talk yesterday, and we're concerned."

My palms start to sweat. *Concerned* is code for alarmed.

"Between your tardies and 'sick days'"—Principal Huxx

air-quotes *sick days* so we all understand she doesn't consider me sick—"your absences are excessive and your grades are suffering."

Shame burns my face. My good grades are the one thing I have going for me. I'm a perfectionist, so that usually works in my favor. I do my assignments over and over again until they're flawless. I sometimes turn in work late because I can't stop perfecting it, but until this year, it hasn't been too much of an issue. Most of my lower school teachers appreciated my careful, tidy papers. And let's face it, in elementary if you're not nibbling on the Play-Doh, you're pretty much acing it. The problem is sixth grade. Teachers take points away for lateness. They expect speed and accuracy, and that's harder to manage. Especially when missed work piles up because of absences and trips to the nurse's office, but I didn't realize my grades were actually *suffering*. Tears sting my eyes.

Dad glances at me, and I quickly blink them away.

"Maybe we should have this meeting in private." Dad's tone and face are neutral. The tightness in his jaw has been erased, as if he's purposely wiped away all emotion now that he fully comprehends why we're here. I guess that's why he's a captain. Calm under pressure. I wonder if I'm adopted.

"I know this is hard for Marvel to hear, but she's in

middle school now. Her grades and her attendance are her responsibility. All her teachers agree." Principal Huxx motions to Ms. Day for confirmation.

Unlike Dad, Ms. Day's an open book. It's clear she's uncomfortable with this ambush, but Principal Huxx is her boss, and like I said, everyone is afraid of her. "Her teachers do feel it's important that Marvel understands the situation as we work toward a solution."

Okay. Message received. Time to go. As happy as I am to spend time with Dad, I don't want to do it in a meeting where Principal Huxx can tell him all the things I don't want him to know. I push back my chair, ready to bolt. It slams into the pea-green wall.

Dad puts his hand on my arm to keep me where I am. "A solution? What's at stake here?"

Principal Huxx meets Dad's eyes. She speaks candidly and quickly, like she's ripping off a Band-Aid. "Her progression to seventh grade."

My insides twist, and my eyes burn. I can't fail sixth grade. All the kids I've gone to school with since kindergarten would move on ahead and leave me behind. I'd be completely humiliated. Even talking about it is mortifying.

As if she hasn't already said enough, Principal Huxx continues, "Unfortunately, she's not in elementary school anymore. The grading system, the attendance, everything adds up and matters. She's lagging in all categories. It's the spring semester. There's not much time left to rectify the situation, and after yesterday, I'm very concerned about her end-of-the-year project, the school play. It's a big percentage of her final grade."

I don't want them to, but tears drip down my cheeks. I turn my head away from Dad, Ms. Day, and Principal Huxx and stare at the puke-colored wall. I'm stunned and frustrated. I try hard to be good at school, but it's tough. There are so many things to get right.

Dad pats my arm. "What does she need to do? I'm sure she can catch up. Marvel's always been a good student."

We both know it's not true. I genuinely like the learning part of school, but I'm bad at all the other stuff that matters—being in the classroom, participation, speeches, plays, friends, lunch. There's a lot more to school and being a student than adults remember. It's not only about turning in assignments on time, and even if it were, apparently I'm also not good at that.

Principal Huxx details the specifics of her plan. "She needs to show up on time each and every day and remain in class the entire time. No late arrivals, early dismissals, or spending the day in the nurse's office. In addition, she'll have to do some extra credit to make up for her missed classwork. Ms. Day will work with Marvel on what she needs to do. Most importantly, she needs to participate in the play. Ms. Day will find a small part for her, something manageable, but she's got to be in it. It's a requirement for all sixth graders," Principal Huxx finishes firmly.

Dad nods as if everything she's suggested is doable. "I think Marvel can meet those obligations."

Ms. Day smiles at me. "We know she can do it."

I'm glad they're confident, because to me, it sounds impossible. There's makeup work, the play, and facing my classmates again after freezing onstage in front of the entire school. To make matters even worse, my go-tos for survival have been yanked away from me. I can't stay home sick, hide out with Skippy, or shorten my days by coming in late or leaving early when worry eats away at me until my stomach hurts. If I lean on my old ways, I'm going to flunk sixth grade, and I really, really don't want to be held back.

The stress of all the things I need to change and get right for promotion to seventh grade makes my chest so tight it feels like an elephant is sitting on it, and my eyes burn with tears again.

The bell rings, signaling the start of the school day.

Ms. Day stands. "Why don't we walk to homeroom together, Marvel?"

I swipe my tears away and stand up.

Dad rises and gives me a hug goodbye. I'm so ashamed

he had to hear Principal Huxx say those things about me, I can barely return it. "Have a good day, sweetheart."

Not likely.

"Let's not be late, Marvel," Ms. Day says, waiting to usher me out of the conference room.

Nope, wouldn't want to be late to class.

10

KERPOW

I think what's hard to understand about me and school is that I don't actually hate it. I know my accumulation of absences, late arrivals, and early exits gives the impression that I do or that I hate other kids. Neither is true. I love to learn new things, and I want friends. It's the pressure not to mess up that makes everything miserable, to get it *all* right—the answers, the words, the clothes, the hobbies, the chitchat. It's a lot to worry about. One misstep and KERPOW, it's over.

I know, I know. Everyone says that's not how life operates, but it does. It just doesn't work that way all the time, so I can't plan for it. Life's gonna get me. The problem is, I never know where, when, or how. That's the on-edge part.

Take today, for instance. When I woke up this morning,

I never imagined I'd be dragged into a meeting with Principal Huxx and learn that I'm one play performance away from failing sixth grade, but out of nowhere that happened and I still haven't recovered. In fact, I may never be able to get into the car to go to school again without having flashbacks and feeling a shame so heavy it's like an anchor holding me in place.

On the other hand, I had lain awake ALL night and spent the ENTIRE day worried about kids teasing me, and went to great lengths to avoid them—jumped up and run out of my classes as soon as they ended, taken strange routes between rooms to avoid other people, and looked down at all times to prevent eye contact (if I can't see them, they can't see me).

To my total surprise, almost no one has said anything about my presentation. Aside from a few snickers, it's like the other kids have forgotten all about me. Only one more class to go, and I'm home free. I'm finally starting to relax and believe Mom's been right for once and no one cares about my speech, which is a huge relief because being on high alert all day takes its toll. When I'm jazzed up, it's hard to eat or focus. My mind is repeatedly attacked by visions of worst-case scenarios that make my stomach drop and roll with queasiness. It's like riding on a roller coaster that I desperately want to get off of, but it refuses to stop.

The great thing is it's Friday, so that means in one hour the weekend starts. I can go home to Butter, Dad, Mom, and Reef and forget all about this place for two glorious days.

I slink into language arts and slide into my chair.

The bell rings, and kids scramble to their seats as Ms. Day takes her place up front.

We sit at round tables in small groups. My group is Addie, Mercedes, and Theo. The three of them are besties, so that's awkward for me. Addie is perfect. Theo is kind, and Mercedes is a chatterbox. It's a good table. One of the better ones, actually, even if we always get in trouble for talking. It's not me, of course. It's them, but mostly Mercedes. Having all of us face one another instead of the front of the room, where Ms. Day stands, is too much temptation for her. Mercedes comments on everything. It's like she live-tweets our school day. I think I got put with them because I'm shy at school. Teachers always do that. They stick the quiet kids with the talkative ones. I don't mind. I like Mercedes's chatter.

Though, our table setup is the reason I don't notice the screen at first.

Mercedes gets the seat that faces the front of the room while Addie and Theo get the side views. I look at the back of the classroom. It usually works for me, but today is atypical. Ms. Day has a surprise in store.

"You were magnificent yesterday!" Ms. Day oozes with first-year-teacher pep.

I don't swirl my body around to look at her because, clearly, she isn't speaking to me and I like to give my neck a break. I sometimes worry the twisting will cause long-term damage to my spine. After all, I'm not part hoot owl.

"You put your best efforts into your projects, and it showed! That's why I'm excited you're going to get a chance to see yourselves, just as the audience did yesterday!"

I whip my head around, and that's when I see the screen. My whole body goes cold.

Ms. Day walks around the room handing out papers. "As you watch, please record each presenter's name along with one compliment and one critique. I'll collect them and compile everything into a list for each person."

Mercedes sticks her hand in the air.

Ms. Day stops by our table and drops four papers in the middle. "Yes, Mercedes?"

"What if we have more than one critique?" Mercedes snatches the handouts and passes each of us one.

Ms. Day pauses near me. "I want you to keep it to one per person."

I put my head on the table like a depressed dog. Eternal video evidence of the most embarrassing moment of my life is the very thing I've been worried about. It's the worst of worst-case scenarios, and it's more awful than I imagined. In hindsight, I'd rather have my classmates tease me than have to face myself on-screen.

Ms. Day kneels down next to me and whispers, "Don't worry, Marvel. I don't plan on showing your presentation unless you want me to."

I shake my head. Ms. Day is banana cakes if she thinks I want anyone, especially myself, to see a replay of my complete full-body meltdown.

She pats me on the back and heads to the front of the room to start the playbacks.

In between presenters, Addie sneaks peeks at me.

She keeps doing it, so I scooch back, creating a cocoon with my arms that allows me to block her out.

"Marvel," Addie whispers, and shakes my shoulder. "You okay?"

I'm not. Not at all. I'm miserable. Just when I was sure everyone had forgotten all about the presentations and I'd almost decided it might be safe for me to move on also, Ms. Day trots out video evidence to jog our memories.

Addie sighs.

I hear the speeches, one after another. Everyone is doing great; so far no one has even gotten tripped up or stumbled over their words.

Theo and Mercedes whisper to each other. It sounds like they're arguing, but I can't really hear them with my head down. Addie finally blurts out, "She's obviously upset about her speech."

I don't lift my head off my arms to acknowledge them.

Mercedes reaches across the table and pokes me. "Theo's next."

"Mercedes," Theo says, "leave her alone."

I sit up to watch him. It feels like the right thing to do since we're tablemates.

Theo went all out for his Steven Spielberg costume. He sprayed his hair gray, wore glasses, and used an old film camera as a prop. Theo's dad is an animator or director or something. That's part of the problem with where I live. Everyone is special.

Up on screen, Theo's doing a great job, but I'm watching Ms. Day. She's not paying attention. She seems very distracted by something in her desk drawer. Oh no. She's texting.

I need her to look up. I'm next. She's got to get over to the computer and fast-forward or stop the recording or do whatever it is she planned to do to skip me.

My eyes bore into her. LOOK UP!

Addie and Mercedes stare at me staring at Ms. Day.

My palms start to sweat, and my heart kicks into high gear. For the love of all that is holy, LOOK UP, MS. DAY!

Theo is focused on his on-screen self. I don't know how he can stand it.

"Is something wrong?" Addie asks.

My voice is pure panic. "I'm next. She's supposed to stop it." The speeches are only thirty seconds long. Even though Ms. Day is a new teacher and pretty young, she's still old in relation to us. She doesn't have the texting dexterity we do. She probably types in complete sentences.

Addie glances at Ms. Day. "Is she texting? Teachers aren't allowed to do that in class."

I nod, helpless.

Addie elbows Mercedes. "Ms. Day is supposed to stop the recording before it gets to Marvel, but she's texting."

Mercedes checks out Ms. Day.

Now we're all staring at her. You would think she'd feel it.

Ms. Day smiles and starts texting again as Theo's speech ends. Ms. Day doesn't notice the speaker on the video change. On-screen, I walk up to the microphone.

I stop staring at Ms. Day and watch the video.

All around me, my entire class is utterly silent as yesterday's horror replays from a completely new perspective—the audience's viewpoint.

I watch myself stumble up to the microphone and stand in front of it. I see my mouth open and close like a guppy as I try to say words and forget all of them. Then I do nothing. Absolutely nothing. I stand frozen while the flashlight goes on and off as if it's yelling, *Speak, Marvel. Speak!*

It's even worse on film. I know it's me, but that girl on-screen makes no sense. I don't know why she's so afraid of everything, even a silly thirty-second speech that other kids ace without an ounce of concern, or how she ended up like that. My heart hurts, and I feel sorry for her because she's in a cage of her own making, frozen in place by her own fears. Fears she collected as sparks and tended until they burst into an inferno.

I ball my hands into tight fists and squeeze as hard as I can to try to hold my tears inside. I don't want to cry in front of my class on top of everything else. It doesn't work.

Tears fall from my eyes.

Addie is the first to react. "Ms. Day!"

Ms. Day's head pops up, the smile still fixed to her face. It takes about two seconds for her to figure out what's happening. She drops her phone into her drawer. The thump echoes. She runs to the computer and starts frantically pressing buttons.

She's already wasted twenty seconds texting, figuring out what was happening, and racing to the computer. By the time she finally presses pause, she freezes me on-screen at thirty seconds, the height of my panic. A mere instant before someone yells, *Get her off the stage!* and Principal Huxx comes to carry me off.

I'm like one of those people from Pompeii, suspended in time at the exact height of my horror.

Jamie laughs. "I'm sorry, but that's hilarious! She's so frozen, she looks like an icicle. No, a snowman. Ha! She's Frosty . . ." He looks around the room to gauge the response to his joke. "You know, like the snowman? Come on! Frosty. It's funny."

"If you have to explain it, it's not funny," Addie snipes, but despite her defense of me, the entire class starts cracking up, even the nice kids, and I feel like crawling into a hole.

Ms. Day clicks off the computer. "Jamie. Principal Huxx's office. Now." She points to the door.

Jamie swings his backpack over his shoulder and high-fives his buddies as he walks toward the door. He's not even sorry. Just before he steps into the hallway, he says, "Later, Frosty."

Ms. Day looks pained.

I put my head back down on the table and hide in my cocoon.

"Ooof, *Frosty* is going to catch on," Mercedes says.

I hear a smack.

"Ouch, Addie, that hurt," Mercedes says, indignant.

"You're making it worse." Addie pats my arm.

"It's not her fault people are mean. I'm just saying—" The bell goes off, interrupting Mercedes.

Everyone bolts for home, except for my table.

I stay where I am, unmoving. I can't leave until everyone is gone.

I feel Addie, Theo, and Mercedes lingering.

"Um . . . should we do something?" Theo whispers.

I understand his confusion. We're tablemates, which makes us acquaintances, not friends. Friends do stuff together. We just sit next to one another in class.

"It's okay, you three. Go ahead and go," Ms. Day says. "Do me a favor and shut the door on your way out, please."

The classroom door closes, and from the sound, Ms. Day pulls out a chair. "Marvel, my deepest apology. That shouldn't have happened. Looking at my phone is not something I normally do, but I've been waiting to hear some news. My sister had her baby. I'm an aunt."

She's obviously excited, so I'm happy for her. "Congratulations." I don't lift my head, and my words are muffled.

"That's kind of you." Ms. Day pauses, and the silence is uncomfortable.

"Can I go home now?"

"Of course."

I wipe my tears away and stand.

See what I mean? Just when I thought it was safe again, KERPOW.

CHEERIOS

By the time I get outside, almost everyone is gone. Only two cars still wait in the car line, mine and a shiny black SUV.

Addie, Mercedes, and Theo make their way to the SUV, talking and goofing around. They've all changed clothes. Addie and Mercedes wear pale blue leotards with black athletic shorts and they've pulled their hair into high, tight ballet buns. Theo's outfit coordinates with them. He wears a T-shirt in the same pale blue color and black shorts. They're a mini dance company.

I used to take ballet with them, back when we were all beginners and our leotard color was white. I loved dance. Unfortunately, my anxiety didn't. I quit after a few seasons. Seeing evidence of their progression (only the advanced dancers get to wear blue) and the three of them hanging out together makes me wish I'd kept going. I'd love to have a group of friends to spend time with after school and to still be dancing.

Of all the ways my anxiety hurts me, the loneliness might be the most painful.

I wait for them to climb into the SUV before going to meet Dad.

I pull open the car door, and Butter tumbles out.

She rights herself and gives her whole body a good shake. Then she notices me. As soon as she does, she starts bleating and wagging her tail.

"You brought Butter!" I'm so happy to see her, I scoop her up and hug her, letting the warmth of her soothe my sadness like heat on aching muscles.

Dad chuckles. "I thought she might brighten your day. But seeing the way she greeted you, I think it made her day too."

She nuzzles her nose under my chin, and I snuggle her, embracing her easy love.

"Ready to get out of here?" Dad asks, and turns the car on.

I scramble into it. I've never been more ready to leave a place in my entire life.

———

The next morning, I find Dad at the stove again.

The house smells like vanilla cake. "Yummy, what are

you making?" I sit down with Butter on my lap, relieved it's the weekend. I get to hang out with her for two whole days, and I don't have to go to school, which is amazing. I *seriously* need a break from that place. The bummer is that, even when I'm away from it, my thoughts wander back there like a homing pigeon.

Worrying is my brain's background music. Sometimes the volume is high, sometimes it's low, but it's never off. I can literally worry about anything, but right now it feels like the current playlist is the same five songs—"Stage Fright," "Everyone Laughed," "Caught on Video," "They Called Her Frosty," "Sixth-Grade Failure"—on a constant loop.

That's what I love about being with Butter. When I'm with her or taking care of her, the volume gets so low, I'm almost free of it.

Dad holds tongs and wears a T-shirt that says *Captain Dad*, a Father's Day gift from a few years ago. He stacks waffles onto a plate and sets them on the table. "My specialty. Remember?"

"Oh, yeah . . . that's right." I actually did *not* remember until he mentioned it. These are the things that bother me. I get mad at myself for forgetting special details. It feels disloyal. I stash *loves to make waffles* away with the other little bits of information I'm collecting. Next time he leaves, I'm going to do a better job of remembering him.

Butter puts her head on the table and sniffs the waffles. I scooch the plate just out of her reach.

"Waffles!" Reef comes downstairs. He's wearing his pajamas and sporting some major bedhead. He high-fives Dad. "I've missed these!"

Mom wanders into the kitchen. She's dressed in her Mom uniform—baseball cap, vintage rock-band T-shirt, and jeans. She kisses Dad on the cheek. "It's really nice to have you home."

"It's the only place I want to be." Dad gives her a one-arm hug because he's still holding the tongs in the other hand.

No one notices me at the table. It's like my family reunion invite went to spam, but I get to watch it all on their social media stories. (#blessed #dadshome #meanddadarebesties)

"Okay, cadets! Let's eat." Dad ushers them to the table.

Mom finally spots me. "Nope. Absolutely not. No goats at the table." Since she left early yesterday, she doesn't know Butter ate her breakfast there already.

"Butter and Marvel can stay, right? Just for a few waffles?" Dad might be in charge of sailors at work, but Mom's commander of us kids.

Butter stretches her neck out trying to reach the plate. She wiggles a leg free and puts a hoof on the table.

Mom points at it. "That's where I draw the line."

I stand and swipe a waffle. "That's okay. I'm going to teach Butter how to walk on a leash this morning anyway."

Mom and Reef look at me like I'm bananas.

"That's weird," Reef says. But he's not paying too much attention. He's looking at his phone under the table.

"Three things." Mom counts points off on her fingers. "One, I'm not sure goats walk on leashes, so set your expectations accordingly. Two, Butter is temporary. Keep that in mind. I don't want you getting too attached. Three, you need to get the posting up online and put posters up *today*. I'm sure her owner is worried sick about her." Mom snatches Reef's phone from him.

Reef sighs, "*Seriously?* Marvel can bring a goat to the table, but my cell phone is banned?" He shoves a forkful of waffles into his mouth and starts chewing.

"No goats OR phones at the table." Mom pours cream in her coffee. "These feel like commonsense rules I shouldn't need to actually say out loud."

I wish Mom would stop reminding me Butter is temporary. Every time I hug Butter, I wonder if it's the last time. I can't imagine not having Butter by my side and agonize over what would happen if I'm not there to protect her. "Mom, I found Butter eating garbage. I don't think anyone except me is worried about her . . . and maybe Dad." He seems to really like Butter, and it makes me feel like we have something special in common.

Mom glances at Dad.

He pretends to be overly interested in his waffles.

I can tell Mom is concerned I'm already too attached, which I am. I can also tell she blames Dad. It's going to be fine, though. Butter is the best thing to ever happen to me. Her terrible owner is never going to find her and take her away because I've devised a foolproof plan to make sure it doesn't happen. It can't. We need each other.

Butter squirms, anxious to get down and play. I hold her a little tighter. "Goats can do anything dogs can do, and they're supposed to be super easy to train." As if to prove me wrong, Butter gets free of my embrace and tumbles to the floor, somehow landing on her feet. She's very catlike.

"O-kay," Mom says, slightly sarcastic.

"She hasn't had any training yet. You can't expect her to know how to behave." When I'm done, Butter is going to be perfect. Mom will be so impressed; she'll insist I keep her, and I can stop worrying about losing her.

I take Butter to my room and let her explore while I google walking your pet goat. I make sure to check on her frequently this time, looking up every couple of minutes. I don't want another math book incident. I already have too many school stressors.

Surprisingly, I get a ton of hits. I click on a couple of videos and absorb the basics.

All I have to do is put the leash on Butter and pull her forward. When she walks, I reward her with a treat, preferably a Cheerio.

I pretty much don't need school. Everything I need to know is on YouTube.

Butter and I go into the garage, and I scrounge around until I find some rope that will work for a temporary leash. I load my pockets full of Cheerios. Then I take Butter to the front yard.

I tie the rope to Butter's collar and gently pull like the video showed.

She FREAKS out. She hops and spins around at the same time. She's a bucking bronco.

I don't understand. YouTube made it seem easy.

I give the leash some slack.

Butter calms down.

I pet her and feed her a Cheerio.

She gobbles it up.

I try again.

Butter freaks again. She's like a fish caught on a line, frantic to escape.

I try three more times. Butter goes bananas EVERY SINGLE TIME.

I plop down on the grass, exhausted. Stupid YouTube.

Addie rolls by on her skateboard. Since I live close to the school, kids are always biking, skateboarding, and hanging out in my neighborhood, which I don't like because every time a kid zooms by I'm reminded of the very place I'm struggling to forget.

Addie notices us and turns around. She stops, steps on the back of her board, and when it flips up, she catches it. Apparently, she's a prodigy and good at everything. "No way! Is that a goat?"

"Yep." I give Butter extra slack in her leash to let her graze. As long as I'm not pulling the rope tight, she's fine.

"She's adorable! Where'd you get her?" Addie sits down next to me and takes off her helmet. Addie is the one person I think of as a friend, but while we're friendly to each other, we're not people who actually do stuff together. I've known her since kindergarten, and I don't think she's ever sat on my lawn before.

Butter stops grazing and comes over to me. She wants attention.

As I pet Butter, I tell Addie about finding her eating garbage, her fainting gene, and protecting her from Jamie and his brother.

"Ugh, he's the worst. No wonder he was so mean yesterday."

We're both quiet for a second, and it's awkward.

"You're not still bothered about that Frosty thing, are you?" Addie snaps off a blade of grass and twists it.

"No." I am, but I don't tell Addie. Somehow confessing

how much it bothers me makes it so much worse and I don't want Addie to feel sorry for me. A pity friendship is way worse than not having one at all.

Addie offers the blade of grass to Butter. "I wish I'd found her. Then I'd have a goat." I know the way she means it, but Addie doesn't need a goat. She has everything else—skateboarding tricks, speaking skills, ballet, lots of friends.

Butter sniffs the grass suspiciously.

"Can I pet her?"

"Of course." I put Butter in Addie's lap.

Addie gently rubs Butter's head and back.

Butter wags her tail.

"Oh my gosh! That's the cutest thing ever." Addie's smile is huge. Butter spreads happiness wherever she goes.

"I know, right? She's amazing." I show Addie how much Butter likes it when I pet her on her belly.

Addie tries it out.

Butter closes her eyes, thoroughly enjoying the attention.

"What were you doing when I first saw you and Butter?"

"Trying to train her to walk on a leash. It's not going great."

I demonstrate.

Addie giggles.

Butter shakes her head and snorts defiantly. I love her,

but she is SOOOO frustrating. I wonder if Mom ever feels that way about me.

Addie thinks for a minute. "What would happen if you made a trail of treats for her to follow?"

I shrug. "It's worth a try. I don't have any other ideas."

Addie makes a line of Cheerios around the lawn.

I hold the rope loosely. "Let's pretend to ignore her." If Butter is anything like me, she won't take the bait, just to prove she can't be manipulated.

Addie and I talk about books while sneaking peeks at Butter. We discover we both love *The Penderwicks* and get sidetracked talking about which characters we like best.

While we're talking, Butter eats one Cheerio, looks around, and eats another.

Butter eats a few more by stretching her neck out as far as it will reach. Man, she's stubborn.

Addie and I wait.

Butter tries to get another Cheerio without walking forward, but it's too far away. She raises her head and sniffs the air.

I hold my breath.

She slowly steps forward and nabs the next treat. Then she takes another step.

Addie and I mime cheering.

Butter walks forward.

To keep Butter moving, Addie rushes ahead of us to drop Cheerios on the ground.

We make circles around the lawn as Butter gets the hang of it.

"She's a quick learner." I feel really proud of her.

"Do you think she's ready for a longer walk?" Addie asks.

Riding high on Butter's success, I don't think before I speak. "Yeah, where to?"

Addie ponders our destination. "Oh, I know! Let's go to the pet store. They have some kittens up for adoption."

I hesitate.

"If they're not busy, the girl who works there will let you hold them. I go there all the time. You could buy a toy or something for Butter," Addie says.

I bite my bottom lip, thinking. Three things occur to me at once. Butter needs a real leash. The trip to the pet store will be a good test of Butter's new skill. If she's mastered leash walking, it proves to Mom how easy she is to train. But what seals my decision is the realization that this is the first time Addie has ever invited me somewhere. "Let me tell my mom. Can you watch Butter for me?"

"No problem."

I run inside.

Mom and Dad are doing the breakfast dishes. "Can I go to the pet store to get a leash for Butter?"

"Alone?" Mom asks, surprised.

I know why she's stunned, but I don't have time to explain it. Addie's waiting, and it feels like something special is happening between us, like we might be going from friendly to actual friends. "With Addie and Butter."

Mom raises her eyebrows, but I can tell she's pleased. She elbows Dad. "Give her twenty dollars for the leash."

Dad hands me the money and smiles. "I thought Butter was temporary."

Mom hits him with a dish towel.

I run out the door.

The whole way to the pet store, Addie walks ahead of us making a trail of Cheerios.

The walk to the store usually takes ten minutes, but it takes Addie, Butter, and me almost forty.

When we finally get there, Addie says, "That was the longest walk of my life!"

"No kidding." Butter might be slow, but she's acing it. I can't wait to show off her skills to Mom.

I start to open the shop door and then stop abruptly.

Addie bumps into me. "What's wrong?"

"I didn't think about Butter. Can she go in?"

"Yeah. We take our dogs all the time." Addie pets Butter.

Dogs. I didn't think about dogs being in the store. That makes me nervous. "How many dogs do you have?"

"Two golden retrievers." Makes sense. Addie's

personality kind of reminds me of a golden retriever. Kind and friendly.

I scoop Butter up. "You think there'll be dogs in there?" I'm rethinking the pet store.

"Probably." Addie doesn't seem bothered at all.

Maybe I should go home. I don't want a dog to attack Butter.

"Don't worry." Addie pushes the door open. "It should be fine. My dogs hardly ever have problems in here." She walks into the store.

Hardly ever is not never. I feel like I'm the only person in the world who thinks about worst-case scenarios.

The door swings shut behind Addie.

She pops her head back out. "You coming?"

I grimace.

Addie laughs. "It'll be fine. I promise. I'll protect you." She grabs me by the arm and yanks me inside.

CANINE ENCOUNTERS

There are no other customers in the pet store. It's just me, Addie, and Butter.

Addie nudges me with her elbow. "See, all good. No vicious attack dogs."

She's right, and the store is awesome. There's so much fun stuff for pet owners, and I almost missed it by not even walking through the door. Another thing I hate about having anxiety is all the stuff it stops me from trying. It's like a Pac-Man gobbling up the fun before it even starts.

Butter squirms.

I hold her tighter.

She rebels by turning into a flurry of hooves, legs, and bleats.

"Okay." I put her down, and it's as if I've released a tornado. Butter's legs splay out in four different directions as she scrambles to get her footing on the slick, polished floor. She's a bouncy ball, going up and down as she tries to stand on her own feet.

Addie cracks up. "Could she be more adorable?"

I smile. "Silly girl." I grab her around the middle to help steady her.

She looks back at me with her light blue eyes, and I swear she wants to say thank you.

"Better?" I ask her, laughing. I slowly let go.

The store clerk comes out from the back. She's a college kid dressed in all black with multiple face piercings. She takes five giant combat-booted steps toward us. "OH! MY! GOSH! THE CUTEST . . . !"

The volume of her voice is so loud it reverberates around the empty shop. Before she can finish her sentence, Butter freezes and tumbles over. She lies on her side, legs rigid. It's the first time she's fainted since the storm, and I feel terrible that I've exposed her to a stressful situation.

I drop to my knees and stroke Butter's side.

Addie kneels down next to her too. "Poor Butter."

"IS THAT A FAINTING GOAT?" Apparently Goth Girl has only one volume setting. Extra loud.

I nod, and my heart flutters. I know I need to say

something about how loudly she talks. Explain that loud noises frighten Butter. Only, it's not easy for me. I'm not used to asserting myself, but I need to speak up for Butter. Without me, she doesn't have a voice.

I hear the words I want to say taking shape in my head as my heart's fluttering turns into rapid flapping. Despite my building nerves, I take a deep breath and force myself to say, "Loud noises scare her, so maybe . . . if you don't mind . . . speaking a little softer?"

And Goth Girl is really nice about it. "Did I do that?" She points to Butter, who hasn't revived yet.

"Maybe . . ." I pause. Feeling buoyed by her kind response, I decide to be more honest. "Yes, the sudden loudness frightened her." I untie the rope from her collar and glance at Goth Girl nervously, waiting for her response.

"Yikes. Sorry. Only whispers from me while you're in the store. I love goats," Goth Girl says quietly.

I'm pleasantly surprised. Being up front about what happened and what Butter needs went over better than I expected. Goth Girl didn't get mad or sad or do anything except agree to speak softer for Butter's sake. More confident people probably get this type of response all the time. But it's a big deal to me. I'm not used to speaking up about things to strangers, especially ones older than me. "I'll introduce you. She'll be up in a second."

As if on cue, Butter moves. I help her get her footing,

and she takes off, checking out everything—the dog food, leashes, bowls, and toys.

I shake my head and laugh. I admire Butter. She doesn't let fear stop her from enjoying life. She might fall over, but she pops up eager to get right back out there. I'm the exact opposite. One bad experience, and I hunker down.

The three of us watch Butter explore for a few minutes.

Finally, Goth Girl sighs dreamily. "I could watch her all day, but can I help you find something?"

"She needs a leash." I hold up the rope as evidence.

Goth Girl shows Addie and me a selection of leashes while Butter explores.

Addie helps me pick out a blue one with a matching collar. "It will go with her eyes."

I hold the leash next to Butter's face. "It's perfect."

"Where did you get your goat?" Goth Girl asks.

"I found her." I look at the price tags on the collar and leash. I have just enough for both.

"What have you done to find her owner?" Goth Girl organizes leashes on the display.

"Nothing yet. I'm going to put up some signs, but I doubt I'll get contacted. Butter's old owner doesn't care about her."

Goth Girl considers me. "How do you know?"

I feel defensive. She sounds like Mom. "It was obvious

when I found her. Her fur was matted and dirty. She was eating garbage and being teased by a group of kids. I mean, who leaves a baby goat to fend for themselves?"

Goth Girl nods empathetically. "Poor thing. There's no explaining some people. But you never know. It might be a misunderstanding. One Fourth of July, I lost my dog. He got frightened by the fireworks and took off. I finally found him a few days later, and he looked like he'd had a pretty rough go of it. I know I did. It was the worst few days of my life."

Clearly, Butter's situation is completely different. "Well, sure, but you're a pet person. I mean look at where you work. I don't think Butter's owner is anything like you."

"Maybe," Goth Girl says.

Addie taps me on the shoulder. "Look." She points to Butter.

Butter approaches a pen with kittens for adoption. She watches them, transfixed.

Goth Girl, Addie, and I wait to see what Butter will do.

At first she stares at the cage. Then Butter's curiosity finally gets the best of her, and she sticks her nose right next to it. A black kitten arches his back and hisses. Butter butts the cage, and we crack up.

She trots over to me. "Had enough of kittens?" I ask, laughing.

She bleats in answer.

I pull her to me so I can replace her old collar with her new one, and clip the leash to it.

As soon as I'm done, the store door opens. A woman with a huge dog starts to enter the store. It's some sort of shaggy beast that weighs at least one hundred pounds.

"Oh, my gosh." I squeeze Addie's forearm. "Is that a woolly mammoth?"

"Wow." Even Addie seems intimidated by the dog's size.

I pick Butter up and watch beast-dog approach. My instincts scream *Run*, but beast-dog blocks the exit.

Despite his size, he's really slow.

When he gets closer, I brace for attack. I curl myself around Butter to shield her from harm and squeeze my eyes shut.

"Um . . . Marvel." Addie taps my shoulder.

"Yeah?" I ask without opening my eyes.

"I think you're all good." I hear a hint of laughter in her voice.

Warily, I open one eye and then the other.

Beast-dog is lying on the ground with his head between his paws.

"Vicious," Addie whispers. Then she loses it, laughing so hard she can barely breathe.

"I matched my fear to his size." I try to be mad, but I can't. It's funny.

"That's an interesting pet." Beast-dog's owner points to Butter.

"I could say the same to you. Mine's a goat. What's yours?" I put Butter on the ground.

Beast-dog's owner is a petite woman with dark brown hair. She smiles at us. "This is Sonny. He's a Newfoundland."

Butter wags her tail as she meets Sonny. She hops around, trying to entice him into playing.

Sonny completely ignores her. He doesn't even lift his head.

Addie pets Sonny. "He's really gentle."

"Most Newfies are, but he's also a therapy dog, so he's extra mellow," Beast-dog's owner says.

"What does a therapy dog do exactly?" I mean, sure, I know the general concept, but I wonder if they have to perform tricks or special tasks.

"Sonny goes places where people might be in anxiety-provoking situations. Sometimes, just having Sonny around can make someone feel better."

Huh. Butter eases my anxiety. "He just needs to hang out and be himself?"

She nods. "But he also has to be well behaved and pass some tests. We mostly go to hospitals, but we've been invited to schools before. Sonny needs to know how to behave in those environments."

This is an interesting revelation. "I didn't know animals were allowed at schools."

"I don't know about all animals. Sonny is a trained therapy dog, which is fairly common. I do have a friend who owns a therapy pig."

"That's cool," Addie says.

Very cool and very interesting. The wheels in my brain start spinning, and I want to ask Sonny's owner a million more questions, but she seems like she needs to get going. As they leave, Sonny moves so slowly, it's like watching paint dry.

When the door closes, I tell Addie, "Well, that huge beast was nothing to worry about."

"I told you so." She doesn't sound smug, just encouraging. "Ready for the Cheerio trail home?"

"Ready!"

Addie drops Cheerios on the ground, and Butter snags them one at a time, making progress toward the door.

When we get close to the exit, Goth Girl whispers, "Come back soon," and waves. I'll definitely be back. The pet store is awesome.

Addie reaches for the door and opens it.

A tiny, silky terrier runs through, barking her head off.

Butter promptly freezes up and collapses.

The terrier plants herself in front of Butter and barks nonstop.

"Get away from her." I jump between the terrier and Butter's still form on the ground.

The terrier lunges at me, trying to nip my ankles.

"Shoo! Get away!" I block the terrier's attempts to get to Butter. I'm afraid the little dog is going to scare her to death.

"Where's that dog's owner?" Addie asks, panicked.

"No idea!" Goth Girl runs to the door and sticks her head out. "WHOSE DOG IS THIS?" She steps back as someone comes to the door.

To my complete horror, Jamie, aka meanest kid in school, walks through the door like he owns the place. "Mine."

"Leash your dog," Goth Girl demands.

"Hold your horses. I'm working on it." Jamie saunters across the store swinging a leash around, taking his sweet time on purpose.

"Hurry up, Jamie! Your dog is trying to bite me." I jump in place as his terrier nips at my ankles in her attempts to get to Butter.

"Calm down. She's too small to hurt you." He snaps the leash on her collar and drags her away from me.

I immediately pick up Butter. "Your dog made her faint," I accuse.

Jamie smirks. "So what? That's what the stupid goat does. She's a fainting goat, remember?" He picks up his growling and snapping dog.

Butter hides her head under my chin.

I cover Butter's eyes to shield her. "Get her out of here, Jamie."

"Yeah, she's freaking out Butter." Addie stands beside me and crosses her arms.

Jamie rolls his eyes. "Ooh, watch out. Attack dog's going to eat Frosty and her stupid goat."

My face flames with embarrassment and anger.

"Don't call her that," Addie says.

"Lighten up, Addie. It's just a nickname. Since when do you care about Frosty anyway?" Jamie tucks his dog under his arm.

Addie glares at him. "Don't be mean."

"All right, that's enough." Goth Girl holds the door open. "OUT!" I'm grateful her volume control is stuck on loud because it seems to intimidate Jamie.

"Relax. I'm leaving. We hate this store anyway." As soon as the door shuts behind him, it gets quiet.

My whole body is shaking. I put Butter down to check her out. She seems perfectly fine. Better than me, actually.

Addie touches my shoulder. "Are you okay?"

I'm not sure. My heart beats so hard it feels like it's going to burst through my chest. "I think so. You?"

She nods. "Jamie's a jerkface. Ignore him. He doesn't know anything."

"Yeah, I know." I turn to Goth Girl. "Thanks for kicking him out."

"I got your back." She fist-bumps me and then Addie. "Just remember, there are no bad dogs, only bad owners." I like her. Too bad I'll never see her again. I can't come back here. Too dangerous.

"Home?" Addie asks.

"Definitely." I've had enough adventure for one day.

LOST CREATURE

I say goodbye to Addie at my gate and watch her skateboard off into the afternoon sunshine. Just before she turns the corner at the end of my street, she gives me one last look and waves like we hang out every day.

I'm not going to lie—the run-in with Jamie rattled me, but being with Addie and Butter made it not so awful somehow. I bend down and drape my arm over Butter's neck. "That turned out okay, huh?"

She bleats at me and pushes her nose into mine. I giggle and take her inside.

When I get into the house, Mom asks, "*So . . .* how did it go with Addie?"

"Fine," I say, giving her nothing. I can tell she's a little too invested in my answer, and I don't want her to get her hopes up. Mine are high enough for both of us.

She sighs, disappointed. "Anything *else* on your agenda today?"

It's obvious she means the Nextdoor posting and the flyers. "I'm going to work on the posters."

"Good answer. I need you to keep in mind that Butter is only with us until we locate her owner or someplace suitable for her to live." Mom's tone is all no-nonsense and come-back-to-reality.

"Sure." I nod agreeably. Mom might feel that way now, but she's going to change her mind. Butter's leash-walking skills improved a lot on the way home. With a little more practice, she'll be perfect, and I can show Mom. Once Mom sees how well-behaved Butter is, she'll let me keep her forever.

"Why do I feel like you're not hearing me?"

I shrug. "Can I borrow your cell phone to take pictures of Butter for the signs?"

"Sure." She hands her phone over.

I take photos of Butter in the garage. The lighting is dim, but that works perfectly for my purposes. I open the photo editor and make a few adjustments. Then I email the pictures to myself and press delete. I can't risk Mom seeing my handiwork.

Butter crawls onto her bed and falls asleep, exhausted from our outing. I leave her in the garage to rest since Dad hasn't finished her enclosure yet.

I return Mom's phone and go to my room.

Once I'm there, I open my computer and make a flyer. I upload the digital version to Nextdoor and press print for three hard copies (hey, I'm conserving our natural resources) to hang up around our neighborhood.

I knock on Reef's door. There's no answer, so I walk in. He's lying on his bed with noise-canceling headphones on and his eyes closed. I poke him in the shoulder.

It's a gentle prod, just to get his attention, but he practically falls off the bed. "What the heck, Marvel!"

I show him the flyers. "Mom said you were supposed to help me hang the posters up."

Reef snatches them out of my hands. "She's going to kill you when she sees these."

In the photo, it's hard to tell exactly what Butter is—cat, dog, cow, fuzzy blob. Anything but a goat, and the text reads:

LOST CREATURE
Color: Black and White
Call Marvel: 455-555-7555

Reef gapes at me. "There's no identifying information on these at all. You can't even tell she's a goat. The photo is too dark and blurry."

"I did my best." Butter needs to be protected from her old owner, not handed back over.

Reef sighs. "Whatever. Let's just get this over with. As soon as I'm done helping you, I get to meet up with Suzanna, so the faster the better."

"Works for me."

I leave Butter at home while Reef and I stick flyers in a few key locations. I put one behind the grocery store, slap another on the underside of a bench, and tack the last notice on the bulletin board in the pizza shop, making double sure it's covered by several other flyers.

Reef flips through the stack covering it. "How's anyone supposed to find that?"

"Think of it as a test. If Butter's old owner truly cares about her, they'll do whatever it takes to find her." If not, Butter is all mine.

"Ridiculous," Reef says, but I know he doesn't really care. He just wants to dump me and go hang out with his girlfriend. "Are we done here?"

"Yep."

Reef walks me home. When we get to the garden gate, he says, "See ya. Wouldn't want to be ya."

I punch him in the arm.

He mockingly rubs his bicep. "Ouch. So painful. How will I ever recover?"

Brothers. I roll my eyes and go through the gate.

Dad's in the garden, standing in front of the enclosure he's built for Butter, grinning. As soon as I get close, he steps aside to give me a complete view of it.

Dad's crafted a pint-sized stable made out of dark, richly colored wood and surrounded by a sturdy fence. On the front is an adorable Dutch door that allows the lower and upper halves to open and close independently.

Stunned at the detail, I walk toward it and peer through the door. Inside is a trough stuffed with sweet-smelling hay and a hook with a water bucket hanging from it. Dad's thought of everything.

"What do you think?" His voice resonates with satisfaction and delight, as if he's given me the perfect gift . . . and he has.

"It's amazing!" I fling my arms around him, overjoyed to have an ideal home for Butter—one that makes my dream of keeping her feel a bit closer.

Dad hugs me back, and I realize he's given me something else too—a special memory of my very own. One that will never fade, no matter how far he travels or how long he's gone.

MAROONED

Monday morning rolls around faster than I expect. As soon as I wake up, my mind recaps all the reasons going to school stinks—failing grades, too many absences, the upcoming play, my extreme stage fright, my new nickname, and my math book. All of it tumbles around my brain like clothes in a dryer, and before I even set one toe on my bedroom floor, I feel sick.

My head hums, my body randomly aches, and my stomach rolls.

I find the thermometer and take my temperature. When it reads normal, I'm utterly shocked.

I wander into the kitchen holding my stomach.

Mom's at the table with a cup of coffee. She takes one look at me and says, "You're going to have to power through, honey. Dad told me about your meeting with Principal Huxx. No more sick days."

"But I could infect people. I think I have a stomach virus." I stick a Pop-Tart in the toaster.

Mom raises her eyebrows.

"What? It's my comfort food." I go to her and lean down so she can feel my head.

She half-heartedly puts her hand on my forehead. "All good."

I scowl at her. I don't trust her assessment. Her fingers barely grazed my skin.

Mom takes a sip of coffee. "Do you want to talk about what's really bothering you?"

It's not easy to share my worries, even with Mom. No one sees the world the way I do, and people always dismiss my concerns in an attempt to make me feel better. It doesn't work. It just makes it hard for me to be honest.

I put my Pop-Tart on a plate and sit down. All weekend, I tried to formulate the best argument for homeschooling and looked for the perfect opportunity to talk to Mom as a last-ditch effort to save myself from having to go back to school. I could never find either and time's run out. "I've been thinking, now is the perfect time to homeschool. Having Butter with us is a unique experience. Animal husbandry is practically a lost art. Now that Dad's home, he could manage my learning and you could leave to go to your landscaping—"

Mom interrupts me. "Dad won't be able to stay home permanently right now. You know that."

I do, but I've been secretly hoping something had changed. I let the reminder of his impending departure uncomfortably settle for a minute, and then forge ahead. "I've been having all these attendance issues, and if I was homeschooled—"

Mom interrupts me again. "Your solution for too many absences is to stop going to school altogether?"

I feel like Mom is intentionally misunderstanding me. "No. I'm just saying, you wouldn't have to stay home with me. You could still go anywhere you wanted, and I could do my learning online. I mean everyone says homeschoolers are the most interesting people. Didn't some kid write a novel—"

Mom interrupts me a third time. I thought she wanted *me* to talk.

"We don't send you to school because we think you need babysitting. We send you to school because we value the education you get there."

"Well, that's a good point. *Am* I getting a good education? The spring semester is mostly focused on the play, which feels . . . unbalanced. What about math and science?"

She puts her hand on mine. "I know you're nervous about the play, but try to look at it as an opportunity. A do-over."

Exactly what I don't need—a chance to make a fool out of myself, AGAIN. "If I mess up the play, which is pretty much guaranteed after the other day, I'm going to fail sixth grade. Mom, I can't . . ."

I abruptly stop speaking as a lump forms in my throat and a vision of Addie, Theo, Mercedes, and Jamie moving up to seventh grade while I stay behind in sixth plays out in my head. Because of the way my school, Bayside Academy, is set up, I'd see them constantly even though I'd be held back. Every time I passed them in the hall, I'd be reminded that I failed. Worse, they'd know I flunked. A knot twists in the pit of my stomach. "That would be awful."

She squeezes my hand and holds it. "You're a good student. Dad and I have faith in you."

At the mention of Dad, the desire to not let him down presses against me. I drop my head and stare at my half-eaten Pop-Tart.

"You can do it. And you and Addie have started hanging out. Don't you want to go to school to see her?"

I don't want to go to school for any reason. I look at Mom. "We went to the pet store together once, and I'm pretty sure that's because she likes Butter." I knew Mom had her hopes up. She needs to adjust her expectations accordingly. I have. My outing with Addie might be a one-hit wonder.

Mom gives my hand a final squeeze, wrapping up the conversation. "Don't sell yourself short."

I roll my eyes. She's such a mom.

"Go get ready. I'll drop you at school today." Mom dumps the rest of her coffee in the sink.

My stomach still hurts, but I get ready despite the aching. Before leaving my room, I crawl under my bed and retrieve my mangled math book. It looks like it's been attacked by a lawn mower. I blow dust off it and shove it into my backpack, hoping whatever lesson is on the page Butter ate never gets taught. Then I go outside to check on her.

Butter's enclosure is perfect. It's cozy and secure. She seems to love it.

I give her some fresh hay and water, glad she doesn't have to scrounge around in trash cans for food anymore. Her life, at least, is better, and that gives me something to hang on to as I head back to the most miserable place on earth.

Mom honks the horn.

I hug Butter around her neck. Her fur tickles my face and prickles my arms. For a split second, I forget my hurting stomach and the reasons for it as my senses fill with the scent of hay and the warmth of her against my skin. "I'll come home right after school, and we'll go for a walk."

Butter nibbles at my ear.

I rub between her ungrown horns.

Mom honks again.

I reluctantly say goodbye to Butter.

As I walk away, she bleats and bleats, hurting my heart. I know exactly how she feels; I don't want to leave her either. Everything feels better when I'm with her.

I grudgingly get in the car and buckle up for a miserable journey.

Mom backs her Prius out of the driveway and steers it toward school. The knot in my stomach expands as we close the gap between home and school. I calculate how much time there is between now and the play—five weeks. I'm not going to be able to keep this up that long.

"Are you sure I have to go?" I ask when I see Bayside Academy come into view. I don't even try to make my voice sound sad and pathetic; it just does.

"You do, honey," Mom says simply, and pulls into the car line. She creeps along until we're at the front of it.

I grab my backpack and give Mom one last forlorn look.

"You got this!" she says encouragingly.

I groan and push open the door. As I step out, she says, "Mr. J organized a friendship group for you. You meet today at lunch."

"What?" I stand on the sidewalk but refuse to shut the car door to keep her from driving away.

"A friendship group. You've done them before. Mr. J suggested another one. It sounded like a good idea, so I signed the paperwork." She smiles as if she's not out to get me.

"Mom! Are you kidding me?" A car behind us honks. (What is it with these suburban parents? Noise pollution is as bad as air pollution, just ask the poor whales tormented by oceanic shipping noise.)

Mom leans over to pull the door closed and says, "Try to be open-minded, honey. New day, fresh start," and slams it.

Wow, Mom. Just wow.

I watch her drive away with the hopeless desperation of a sailor marooned on a deserted island. When she finally fades out of sight, I head into school.

I weave through the halls, making my way to class. I have social studies first period, but one of the weird things about my middle school is the schedule. It rotates. Some days, we start with first period and other days we end with it. Sometimes third period is after lunch and fifth period is before. Other days, it's flip-flopped. The only dependable thing about the schedule is that it's different every day. It's very weird and causes me a lot of stress. I constantly worry I'm going to mess up and go to the wrong class at the wrong time. Both my math and science teachers have sixth- through eighth-grade classes and my biggest fear is that I'll stumble into a classroom full of eighth graders by mistake. That's why, at almost the end of the year, I'm still hanging on to my worn-out schedule like a life preserver.

I pause outside my math class door and pull out my schedule just to make sure I actually do have the class I think I do. I smooth the creases so I can read the writing and run my finger down the list of my classes. Yep, as I suspected, math's first.

"Yo, Frosty. Still lost in May?"

I look up and see Jamie's brother, Matt, and an entire squad of eighth graders behind him. "What?" I say stupidly. Curse Jamie and his stupid nickname for me.

"Still lost in May, Frosty?" he repeats, as if my *what* was an invitation to repeat his words instead of a declaration of disbelief at his comment.

Someone behind him says, "No way, man. That's Frosty, the girl who froze onstage?"

"Yeah," Matt says, laughing.

"Best assembly ever!" The kid whips out his phone and scrolls. "Check out this text chain. Someone caught Huxx carrying her offstage on video . . ."

Holy smokes! Heat shoots through my entire body, making my face turn scarlet.

He says more, but I don't hear it because I shove open my math class door and tumble inside. Good grief. I'll never be able to walk down the halls without being laughed at now that I'm on an EIGHTH-GRADE TEXT CHAIN. That's literally my worst of worst-case scenarios.

I put my head on my desk, trying to hide from the world. I *will* myself to not sob. I'll never make it through the last twenty-five days of school if I start crying now.

My math teacher, Mrs. Spikes, walks in and unceremoniously gets started. "Eyes up, ears on, books open. Page two hundred and forty-three, everyone."

I drag my head up because getting in trouble for keeping it down would be way worse and pull out my math book. I flip through it. I have pages 242 and 245, but no page 243 or 244. That's the one Butter ate, so I can't follow along with the lesson or do the homework that's sure to be assigned.

I sigh and settle in for an absolutely fabulous day at school.

FRIENDSHIP GROUP

During lunchtime, I reluctantly go to Mr. J's office for the friendship group as ordered.

Friendship group sounds *so* innocent and *so* friendly, but it's a sham. First off, friendship groups are for little kids—kindergartners through fourth graders. NOT middle schoolers. Second off, it's a setup. Groups are organized to help one kid (we all know in this case it's me) become more socially acceptable. Usually, they take four kids from different, carefully curated social statuses and have them meet once a week. The adults have high hopes for these groups and the best of intentions—more empathy for one another and new, exciting budding friendships, but it NEVER EVER works that way. I know. I'm a bit of an expert. I've participated in several.

"Welcome, Marvel! Come on in." Mr. J holds his door open.

I settle into my favorite chair. I don't mind talking to Mr. J. In fact, I like it, but I'm resentful about this group. I need less peer-to-peer interaction, not more.

"We have a few minutes before everyone gets here. How are you feeling about things? I know the last few days have been rough." Mr. J is one of the only people who asks *me* questions about how *I'm* feeling. Most other people like to tell me how I'm feeling or how to fix what I'm feeling.

I pick up one of the fidgets Mr. J strategically places around his office and play with it. I consider telling him about the eighth-grade text chain and my new nickname, but I decide against it. Tattling might make the teasing worse, so I tell him part of what's bothering me. "I'm really worried about the play and freezing up again."

Mr. J nods. "I'm sorry you're feeling that way." That's another great thing about Mr. J; he never tries to fix me. He just listens. He pauses for a moment and lets the silence sit between us.

I half-heartedly manipulate the fidget, sifting through my thoughts. None of them are very comforting until I land on an image of Butter in her enclosure. I can't wait to get home to see her.

He glances up at the clock. "The other students will be

134

here in a second, but let me know if there's some way I can support you at school."

"Thanks." I'm probably going to need to take him up on that offer because I'm not sure how I'm going to manage the next five weeks on my own.

Someone knocks on Mr. J's door even though it's open.

"Welcome!" Mr. J says. "Come in! Come in!"

Kiera and Kylie, two girls from my grade who look oddly similar, grab chairs and sit down. We all know the drill.

Our school loves these groups. The typical mixture is one kind-hearted, gentle soul (me); two medium-hearted, popular kids (Kiera and Kylie); and one other kid (TBD). They call it a friendship group, but the goal is social skills for the outliers. Friendship groups are like reading levels. The grown-ups can call it whatever they want; us kids know the truth.

In unison, Kiera and Kylie say, "Hi, Marvel."

I wave at them. I don't mind Kiera and Kylie, but we don't have much in common. They're majorly into boy bands, lip gloss, and matching outfits, but differences make the world interesting, so I don't hold it against them.

We stare at one another for a few minutes while we wait for our fourth person. I can tell Kiera and Kylie don't want to be missing out on the great things that happen during lunch for people like them. They keep wistfully glancing at the door as if wishing for escape and don't talk. My embarrassment at being the reason they're stuck here grows like a weed, getting thicker and thicker with the lengthening silence.

Just when it starts to get so weirdly awkward it's almost unbearable, my worst nightmare joins us.

Jamie shoves open the door and stomps in like he owns the place. "What's up, Frosty?"

I wince and glare at him. You've got to be kidding me. Out of all the people in the sixth grade to invite to my friendship group, they somehow landed on my bully and thought, *Pick him*.

"Jamie, we talked about safe spaces," Mr. J says kindly.

Jamie spies a beanbag and plops into it. He sinks all the way down, hitting the floor. "Whoa."

I feel smug. The beanbag is the worst place to sit. It looks comfy, but the beans are so beaten down by over-use there's no poof left. If Jamie wasn't such a meanie, I would have warned him.

Mr. J motions to a chair. "Feel free to move, if that would be more comfortable."

"Nah, I'm good," Jamie says, playing it cool.

I roll my eyes. Ridiculous.

"Marvel, safe spaces." Mr. J says.

Me? I'm queen of safe spaces.

"I think you've all been in a friendship group before,

but just in case you don't remember the basics. There's no goal. We simply carve out this time for you four to hang out, play a board game, chat . . . really just relax in a safe space for the twenty minutes we've set aside. And because this is about you all and not me, I'm just here to observe, occasionally facilitate, or answer questions." Mr. J finishes his introduction, then leans back in his chair relaxed and thoughtful, letting us take the lead.

Kiera and Kylie stare at their Converse sneakers.

Jamie tries to find a comfortable position in the bean-bag without being obvious.

I fiddle with the fidget and stare at Jamie.

But none of us talk.

After five minutes, I sigh. Loudly. This silence could go on forever. Mr. J's tolerance for quiet is extraordinary, and the four of us have zippo in common.

As I watch Jamie struggle in the beanbag, I'm reminded of Sonny, the Newfoundland. Like Sonny, Jamie is over-grown. He's definitely too big for that beanbag.

Thinking about pets makes me long for Butter and the way I feel around her. She makes every situation happier and easier. Even calling her to mind eases my stress slightly and makes this horribly uncomfortable situation a tad more tolerable. If I had her physically with me, school might be bearable. Out of nowhere I blurt, "What do you think about therapy animals?"

"You mean like seeing eye dogs?" Kylie asks.

I shrug. "I was thinking more about comfort animals, but I'm not exactly sure of all the differences."

Mr. J seems surprised by the sudden introduction of this topic. He's probably stunned any subject has come up at all. He had to know this group was doomed from the start, but he doesn't let it show for long. "I can help clarify. Emotional support animals and service animals are different. A service animal is a special designation for highly trained dogs and miniature horses. Emotional support animals can be any pet that brings their owner comfort."

"Any pet?" I ask. "Even something unusual?"

"Technically, yes," Mr. J says.

Jamie wiggles in the beanbag chair. "My dad says it's a scam for people who want to sneak their dogs into grocery stores and take them on airplanes for free."

"I don't agree with that at all!" Kiera turns on Jamie, unusually passionate. "The lead singer of P.O.P. has an emotional support dog named Apple that he takes everywhere with him. He has a flying phobia and stage fright. Without Apple, we wouldn't have his music."

Now I get the connection.

"I love P.O.P. Did you know Apple has her own social media accounts?" Kylie asks.

"Of course." Kiera hits Kylie on the leg like she's suddenly been struck by brilliance. "Oh. My. Gosh. I have the best idea! Marvel should get an emotional support dog like Apple to help with her issues."

The word *issues* hits me like a punch. It melts down my whole being, everything I am, to a single molecule—anxiety—and leaves nothing else. It makes me angry that everyone at school only notices the very worst part of me. I want things to be different—me to be different.

"Yeah, how exactly are you going to get through the school play, *Marvel*?" Jamie emphasizes my name, making it clear that I'm the only person there with a problem.

I glare at him because he's right.

He starts to hum "Frosty the Snowman," and my face flames.

"Jamie. Safe space," Mr. J says.

Yeah, Jamie. SAFE SPACE!

The bell rings.

Mr. J pats his knees. "Oh, boy! That went quick—"

Kylie and Kiera jump up and walk out the door. They whip their phones out and scroll as they walk. Most likely looking at Apple's social media accounts.

Jamie heaves himself out of the beanbag and follows them out the door.

"Great conversation, everyone," Mr. J says to their backs.

I wait for them to get out of earshot. I need to talk to Mr. J.

As much as I dislike Jamie, he's right about one thing—I

need to figure out how to survive the next twenty-five days of school plus the play or I'm going to fail. And if the only help grown-ups have to offer is a torturous friendship group, I have no choice but to take matters into my own hands.

Desperate times call for desperate measures.

Mr. J goes back to his chair. "Thanks for showing up today and getting the conversation going. We needed that jump start."

"You're welcome. I was wondering . . ." I begin nervously and then pause. Ever since I met Sonny on Saturday, I've been daydreaming about a way to make my school day more bearable, but I'm afraid to voice it.

"Do you want to ask me something?" Mr. J encourages.

I gather my resolve and continue. "Could you tell me more about emotional support animals? I might want one."

"That's an interesting thought." Mr. J considers me.

"Do you need to do something special to get one?" I ask.

"Not really. Any pet can be an ESA if they bring their owner comfort, but some people get a note from a therapist to register their pet if that's something they'd like to do."

I *definitely* want that. Registration sounds official. "Can you write those notes?" I ask.

"I suppose I can."

"Would you write a note like that for me?" I ask tentatively.

Mr. J regards me. "A comfort pet is a big decision. You need to find the right candidate and make a commitment to the animal."

I already have the perfect candidate—Butter. Everything about my life is better with Butter. When she's with me, I'm happier and more confident. Less stressed and more relaxed. If she could only come to school with me, I'd feel that way at school too, and it would solve all my problems.

I need that note.

My heart starts pounding a million miles a minute, nervous to ask for the note. "*Would* you write a note like that for me . . . now?"

Mr. J suppresses a smile. "That's putting the cart before the horse, don't you think?"

My throat tightens, embarrassed he doesn't agree instantly. I clear it. "Maybe . . ."

"A support animal is something you need to talk over with your family first."

With that note and an official registration, Principal Huxx will have to allow Butter to come to school with me, so I take a deep breath and make myself try again. I cannot make it through one more day without her. "Yes, but it would be nice to have the note now. That way, I'm ready the moment the perfect candidate becomes available."

Mr. J smiles. "I do believe you're advocating for yourself and proactively seeking a creative way to manage your anxiety. I'm not sure what's prompted this change, but I'm glad to see it."

"Really? So, you think the note is a good idea?"

"Well . . ." He seems like he's debating with himself. Finally, he says, "I guess it can't do any harm. I'm proud of you for taking a risk. If your parents don't want you to get a pet, they'll let you know."

I bubble with happiness. "They absolutely will. You know my mom."

Mr. J smiles. "Yes, I do." He scribbles a note on his letterhead and puts a sticky on top asking Mom to call him.

I leave Mr. J's office smiling and dump the sticky into the first trash can I pass.

SELF-HELP

As soon as I get home, I make a beeline for Butter. I don't even stop inside the house to drop off my backpack. I go straight to the garden gate and push it open.

Dad's back there with Butter, and when I see the two of them, my eyes practically bulge out of my head and I stop in my tracks.

I can't help it. They're so . . . funny.

Dad hunches over a woodworking project that looks like a sandbox, but I know it is a vegetable planter for Mom because I heard them discussing it. It's almost done, and he moves quickly between tasks, sanding the sides and occasionally checking it with a level, which would be normal enough if it wasn't for Butter.

She stands on Dad's back, peering over his shoulder like she's trying to learn the art of carpentry. Despite Dad's constant movement, she balances on her precarious perch as gracefully as a surfer while he ignores her, working intently, as if piggybacking a goat is something he does every day.

I burst out laughing.

Butter hears me giggle and looks in my direction. She leaps off Dad's back and bounces toward me like I've just returned home from a long deployment, which I feel like I have.

I dump my backpack onto the ground. With it, I let go of everything it represents—the teasing, the anxiety, the insecurity—and scoop Butter up in my arms, reuniting with her.

She presses her muzzle into my cheek, giving me goat kisses.

Dad stands. "How did school go today, kiddo?" The warmth of his greeting wraps around me and tempts me to open up to him. Confess everything. Tell him about my momentary victory with Mr. J and how things went rapidly downhill afterward. Admit that Jamie thinks I'm such a loser that he started a campaign to make his nickname for me stick by humming "Frosty the Snowman" every time I passed by him. Own up to the fact that the other kids must feel the same way because by the time last period rolled around, several of Jamie's buddies had started to do it too. Or that I know tomorrow will be way worse because that's how these things go, which is why I need to take Butter to school with me to survive. But I don't share any of it.

Instead, I shrug noncommittally and keep the trials of my day from him because I can't bear him seeing me through Jamie's eyes. Nor can I fess up to my plan for Butter. He might put a stop to it before I even get a chance to try it out, so I avoid it all by changing the subject. "Thanks for hanging out with Butter," I say, and carry her over to Dad.

He pets her, and she leans her face into his hand, loving the affection. "She seemed like she needed some company. She's a nuisance, though," he says with a fondness that contradicts his words.

I grin at him, letting him know I'm in on his secret. "Right . . . a total nuisance."

Dad winks. "That's my story, and I'm sticking to it. Especially if your mom's listening."

I laugh. "Don't worry. I won't rat you out. I can't believe Butter managed to stay on your back while you were working. She's got amazing balance."

"That she does," Dad says, smiling proudly at Butter with an approval I take personally. "Have a few minutes to help me out?"

"Sure." I loosen my grip on Butter, and she leaps to the ground with impressive agility. "Is that Mom's vegetable box?"

"Yep." Dad hands me one end of a measuring tape and walks backward. He writes his measurements on a slip of paper and does some quick calculations. "But . . . one box will never be big enough. Apparently, your mom's attempting to grow enough food to feed the entire neighborhood or start a farmers market. Honestly, I'm not sure which. All I know is I need to build a second one." He stuffs the slip of paper and pencil in his shirt pocket. "I'll be right back."

Dad goes into his toolshed and comes out carrying an armload of wood. He sets it down next to the first box. "Want to help me build it? It won't take long."

"Sure," I say, pleased with the unexpected invitation. I check my watch. If I'm going to take Butter to school with me, I need to prepare, but there are a few hours before dinner. I should have time to do both, and I want to spend this time with Dad.

He gets the project set up, and we get started.

It's nice working alongside him with Butter bouncing between us.

She seems completely at home and confident. She doesn't even flinch when Dad or I pound a nail. "Butter's doing great with the hammering. I guess she's okay once she gets used to something," I say, once again impressed by her adaptability.

Dad nods. "I noticed that too. She's quite the little trouper."

Butter glances between us and then bleats as if she knows she's being complimented.

Dad and I chuckle.

He hands me the final nail for the vegetable box and the hammer. "Want to do the honors?"

"Sure." I take the tools from him, weirdly flattered. It's only a dumb nail for a simple box, but it feels like we're building something more important than a planter.

Dad bends over to hold the boards in place for me. The paper he calculated the dimensions on falls out of his shirt pocket and drifts to the ground.

Butter pounces and snatches it up. Before either one of us can stop her, she chews and swallows. "Oh, Butter," I say.

Dad laughs. "That goat has a craving for paper. This morning she tried to eat my to-do list."

I shake my head like an indulgent parent. "I know." I give the nail the final taps and step back to admire our work.

Dad drapes an arm over my shoulder. "That's a job well done. You're a better helper than that rascal."

"Glad I'm more helpful than a goat," I joke. "I'm going to

take Butter for a walk, but I need to get something from inside the house. Can you watch her for a bit longer?"

"You got it."

I dash inside and go into my room. I grab Butter's leash and my birthday money, then run back to the garden.

"Okay. Ready." I put Butter's leash on and begin to lead her out of the garden gate.

"Marvel?"

"Yeah, Dad?"

"Where are you off to?"

"The pet store."

"Alone?"

I reach down and scratch Butter's ears, stealing a bit of her confidence. "Nope, with Butter."

A pleased smile lights up Dad's face. "Sounds good. Be back in time for dinner."

"I will." I don't plan to be at the pet store long at all. I actually never imagined I'd be heading back there after my run-in with Jamie, but they have something that I need desperately enough to brave it—a red vest. If Butter is going to go to school with me, she needs a medical vest. Something to show her ESA status, and I remember seeing something like that when I was there with Addie.

As we walk to the pet store, Butter bounces along beside me. She's only been leash-walking a few days, but she's already gotten the hang of it. Every few feet, I reward her with a Cheerio, but I don't have to lay down a trail of them anymore to encourage her to walk.

When we get to the pet store door, I pick Butter up and push the door open a smidge so I can peek inside to scan for dangers like vicious dogs, suspicious people, loose cats, or something else that might be problematic. But only Goth Girl is inside, so I squeeze Butter to my chest to keep her from fainting in case Goth Girl forgets to keep her voice down.

As soon as Goth Girl sees us, her eyes light up with excitement, but she doesn't yell. She waves instead.

I wave back and put Butter down.

Goth Girl comes over to us and whispers, "Glad to see you two again. I think you might be my favorite customers."

"Thanks," I say, genuinely touched. I like her too. She's a bit quirky with her voice volume stuck on loud, but I'm not a typical kid either. My eccentricities are just a little more hidden.

She scratches Butter's ears. "Can I help you find something?"

"I need an ESA vest for my goat."

"I've seen a lot of different ESA pets in my time at the store, but I must confess, she's the first goat. I guess this means her old owner never showed up?"

I don't like the reminder that Butter used to belong to

someone else or the squirmy feeling I get in my stomach at the thought of Butter having another owner who might swoop in and try to take her away. Butter belongs to me, not someone else. "Nope. She's all mine."

"I'm glad you get to keep her. I can tell she's special to you. We have some ESA harnesses that might work over here." Goth Girl leads me to a display and starts shifting through the vests. "Hmm . . . it looks like we only have larges and extra large. I think she needs a small. Let me check our inventory."

Disappointed, I follow Goth Girl over to the checkout desk, where she gets on a computer and types quickly. "We don't have anything in this store, but our other location has one. It's not too far. You can catch a bus at the stop across the street and be over there pretty fast. I do it all the time. Want me to call and ask them to put it on hold for you?"

I bite my bottom lip, thinking. I really want that vest, but the bus is out of the question. For starters, I have Butter with me. I doubt the bus diver will let her on. Then there's also a billion other concerns—making sure I get on the right bus going in the right direction, having exact change, pressing the stop button at the perfect moment (not too soon, not too late), finding a bus back home.

"It's pretty simple," Goth Girl says, noticing my hesitation.

For her maybe.

I really want that vest, but I can't get on a bus. I'll have to figure something else out. "I'm not allowed to ride the bus," I tell her to cover up the real reason I can't go over to the other store.

"We do have these." Goth Girl shows me a selection of name tags. One has a red medical-looking symbol in the middle with the letters ESA and the words *emotional support animal protected under federal law* printed around the outer edge. "I can engrave this with your goat's name and your information."

It looks very official, and I really like the words *protected under federal law*. It's something that might impress Principal Huxx. "That would be great!"

She takes the tag over to a special machine and engraves Butter's name, then mine, onto the back of the tag. She hands it to me. "It's perfect!"

I slip it into my pocket and head home with Butter.

After tucking Butter into bed, I go to my room and google how to register an emotional support animal. A gazillion sites pop up. I scroll down until I find the one I want.

I only need the letter from Mr. J to qualify Butter as an ESA and I have the tag for her collar, but I want us to be super-duper official by joining an ESA registry. Once I do, I'll be able to print a certificate.

I fill out the online form, and it's going swimmingly

until I get to the payment section. I have the money. I just don't have a credit card.

I groan. If I ask Mom or Dad for a credit card, they'll wonder what I'm up to, and I don't want to alert them.

I tap my fingers on my desk while I think about options. I finally land on a solution. Only it's not a sure thing because it hinges on the goodwill of my teenage brother.

I go to his bedroom door and knock.

"Go away."

I want to say something snarky, but I can't chance making him mad. "How do you know it's not Dad or Mom?"

"Osmosis," he shouts through the door.

I throw up my hands. That doesn't even make sense.

"Please. I have a two-second question." I try not to sound too desperate. Big brothers and wolves can smell weakness.

"No," Reef says.

I stick my tongue out at the door and then say, "There's money in it for you." I'm a saver. Reef is a spender. I'm sure I'll end up supporting him one day.

"Ugh. Fine, but make it quick."

I open his door a crack and stick my head in. "I need to borrow your credit card."

He narrows his eyes at me. "Why?"

"No biggie. I just need to buy something for Butter. I have the cash right here." I show him my twenties.

"Ask Mom." Reef puts his headphones on.

"Mom and Dad are busy." He doesn't hear me. "REEF!" He rips his headphones off. "WHAT!"

I deep breathe to center myself. I'm more responsible than him, yet he gets a credit card, a cell phone, and a driver's license. Life is so unfair. "Mom and Dad are busy. If you give me your credit card, I'll pay you ten dollars over what I spend." I set crisp birthday twenties on his desk.

"Fine." He pulls his credit card out of his wallet and flings it at me.

Rude, but since he's the only person I can borrow a credit card from, I keep my opinions to myself. "Thank you," I say sweetly, and close the door.

I go back to my computer and pay for the registry. Click, click, click and it's all done.

I run into Mom's office and pull the certificate off the printer. It has Butter's name, her goat breed, and my name as her owner. I stare at it, transfixed and a bit giddy. I'm almost ready.

I only have one more thing to do—make a vest.

I hunt around the house looking for something red that I can fashion into an ESA vest for Butter. I plow through all my drawers, but red's not my color. I mostly wear muted tones because I prefer to blend into the crowd, not stand out.

I scan our entryway cubbies and check the hall closet,

but I'm not having any luck there either until I spy Reef's soccer bag.

I dig around inside it and find the perfect thing—Reef's scrimmage pinnie.

I shake it out and hold it up. The color is the right shade of medical red. It's made out of nylon, so from a distance, the fabric looks like the vests at the store, and it has Velcro tabs to tighten the sides. It's a little too long for Butter, but I think I can fix that.

I sneak it into my room. I use scissors and duct tape to alter it to fit Butter. Then I add the final touch by stenciling *ESA* in clear block letters on two strips of reflective duct tape and attach them to Butter's vest.

I pull up a picture of an ESA vest online and check my version against the image. It's not an exact match, but it's close enough that I'm proud of it.

I lay out Mr. J's letter, the ESA certificate, the ESA name tag, and the vest to look at them all together. The combination screams official. Even Principal Huxx will be impressed.

As I stare at my handiwork and imagine taking Butter to school, a lightness overtakes me. I'm a hot-air balloon rising.

For the first time in my life, I'm excited to go to school.

MY ESA

I'm already up and dressed when Mom comes into the kitchen. She sees me at the table eating breakfast and does a double take. "You're ready to go early. Is there some sort of special occasion I don't know about?"

"No. Why do you ask that?" I hear the defensive shiftiness in my voice and try to smooth over my tone with a smile.

Mom's eyes narrow with suspicion, and she scrutinizes me as she pours herself a cup of coffee. "What's suddenly made you an early riser?"

"I can get up early."

"Yes. For weekends and vacation days, but never for school."

Sometimes I wish Mom didn't know me quite so well.

I hop up and start clearing my dishes to avoid her piercing gaze. "I decided to walk to school today."

Mom touches my forehead. "Are you feeling okay?"

"Very funny. I'm fine. Just trying something new." She's making me so nervous with her mom intuition that I have to get out of the kitchen before I confess my plan to take Butter to school with me or chicken out altogether. I grab my backpack and head for the door.

Mom stalls me with another question. "Is Addie walking to school with you this morning?"

Jeez, Mom. No pressure. "No. One trip to the pet store together didn't magically make us besties." I wish it did.

Mom holds up her hands. "Just asking. Whatever has motivated this change of heart, I'm all for it. Call me from the office if you need me." Mom kisses my cheek.

"If I had—"

She interrupts me. "I know, if you had a cell phone. You're a broken record."

Sometimes Mom makes no sense. "What's a record?"

Mom gives me her epic eye roll, which is annoying because it's a kid thing and she stole it. Now I can't use it on her. "Bye, Marvel."

"Bye, Mom."

I go out to the garden, and once I'm inside Butter's enclosure, I relax since I'm not concerned about Mom wondering what I'm up to. She's used to me taking care of Butter before school.

I dump Butter's vest and name tag out of my backpack. I snap the new ESA tag onto her collar, loving how important and legitimate it looks.

Next, I tackle her vest. I slip it over her back and attempt to Velcro it together, but Butter doesn't let me. She's too curious about it. She nibbles the edges and tries to shake it off.

It never occurred to me that she might not want to wear the vest.

I pull it off and soothe her, stroking her head and back. "It's okay."

She nips my nose and then goes to her food trough. She pulls a huge chunk of hay out of it and stares me down while she chews.

I hold the vest out. "This is your vest. I made it for you. If you wear it, you can come to school with me," I coax.

She turns her head away, snubbing me.

"Butter! Silly girl." I pull her toward me and slowly slip the vest over her back, making sure to pet her at the same time.

She holds still but curls her head toward me and gives me a pained look, as if she's put out by the indignity of wearing a garment.

"Don't look at me like that. This vest means you're an

emotional support animal. That's super special. You get to go places other pets don't. Like to school with me, and I really need you there. Lately, it's gotten even harder than it used to be." I sigh and lean my cheek on her back, thinking about all of it. The teasing, the play, the makeup work. It's overwhelming.

Butter nudges my shoulder with her nose as if to say *continue*, so I lift my head and share what I've been reluctant to say out loud to anyone else. "If I mess up and get held back, failure will be stamped all over my report card, labeling me. It won't be something I secretly worry about anymore. It will be something I am. I can't be a failure on top of everything else."

I pause, letting the stillness of Butter's enclosure absorb my words. Somehow, voicing my fear to her makes it less scary because it gets it out of my head and into the air, where it can blow away instead of taking root in my brain like a redwood seed.

I start talking again as I gently work the Velcro straps around her stomach and adjust them until they're tight enough. "But if you're there, I think I can do all the things they want me to because you make everything better."

I let go of Butter and step back slowly to see how she reacts.

She sniffs the vest a few times and shakes, but when it

doesn't come off, she bleats and goes back to eating hay, apparently no longer bothered by it.

I watch her munch away, admiring her. She looks adorable and extremely official in her ESA uniform.

I let her finish breakfast while I gather up my backpack and check to make sure the coast is clear, glad Dad is already at an appointment and will be there most of the morning. Once I confirm none of my other family members are lurking outside or looking out the windows, I sneak Butter out of the garden.

She prances beside me, adorable and spunky. I'm so proud of her. Every so often I reward her with a Cheerio just because she's that amazing.

When we get to the field, it's still very early and it's deserted except for an outdoor exercise class filled with senior citizens, who, unlike eighth graders, aren't scary at all.

I wave at them and plow ahead.

I've always thought of the field, the divide between my house and the school, as a vast gulf that I hate crossing because it *feels* daunting. Logically, I know my fear doesn't make sense, but I've never been able to shake it.

Today is completely different, though. I'm so focused on Butter that not only does the walk go fast. It *feels* fast.

For the first time, I see the field through a completely different lens—one that's not clouded by anxiety—and my world shifts for the better. The distance between my house and school is no longer far or scary; it's just a walk. This realization is an eye-opener, and it's all thanks to Butter.

I reach down and pet her.

We walk onto campus and go straight up to homeroom.

After getting ready last night, I wondered if I should check Butter in at the office or ask Principal Huxx for permission before taking her to class with me, but after reading over the ESA paperwork, I decided I didn't need to do either. Butter is a registered ESA. That means something. *Protected by federal law* is even printed right on her name tag. And technically, Mr. J already gave me permission, so we're covered. It's also convenient because, to be honest, I don't want to talk to Principal Huxx about Butter or anything else. She's super scary and she's not what I consider an empathetic person, so it's best if Butter and I go about our business and avoid her at all costs.

Adhering to that theme, I've timed our arrival so we'll get to my classroom before anyone else shows up. We're so early, Ms. Day isn't even at school yet.

I take Butter to my table and sit down with her to wait for what's next.

Butter starts to doze.

She's so warm and snuggly, I get a bit sleepy too.

I'm starting to do head bobs when Addie, Mercedes,

and Theo barge into the classroom in the middle of a vehement debate.

"Being director is a big responsibility," Mercedes says, sighing so forcefully, her bangs blow up and fall back down.

"Of course it is! You're going to be amazing." Addie pats Mercedes's shoulder.

"But I need to be prepared," Mercedes says.

"*You* might need to be prepared, but that doesn't mean *I* have to get up at the crack of dawn," Theo says, exasperated.

"But you're the stage manager. We need regular meetings," Mercedes argues.

Theo yanks on his backpack straps. "We don't even know what play we're doing yet! What kind of meetings can we be having?"

Finally, Addie notices me. "What are you doing here so early?"

Butter is snuggled in my lap, partially hidden by the table. I turn in my seat, revealing her. "I wanted to get Butter settled."

"No way!" Theo comes toward us. "Is she here for a special visit?"

"She's going to be joining me every day. She's my ESA, emotional support animal." I put Butter on the floor so they can meet her.

Theo sits down near Butter. "What a cutie-pie."

"Lucky! I can't believe Principal Huxx let you bring her," Addie says.

"Mr. J gave me permission. She's protected by federal law." I show Addie the ESA tag.

"That's amazing. I want to bring a pet to school." She sits on the floor next to Butter and strokes her.

"Well . . ." I say, not sure how to explain that Butter isn't just a pet. She's serving a purpose.

Butter presses her head into Addie's hand, enjoying the attention.

"I want some of that," Mercedes says, and leans in close to pet Butter. Her hair falls into Butter's face and dangles in front of it like a toy.

Out of nowhere, Butter lunges for Mercedes. She grabs a chunk of Mercedes's hair with her teeth and pulls.

Addie and Theo jump up and back away.

Mercedes screams.

Butter panics, releases Mercedes's hair, and tumbles on her side. Her feet stick straight out, and she doesn't move.

Mercedes scrambles away.

We all stare at Butter. It looks like she has rigor mortis.

"Did I kill her?" Mercedes asks.

"By screaming?" Theo's tone is sarcasm to the tenth power.

Before I can explain, Butter hops to her feet and wiggles her body, shaking off her fainting episode.

Mercedes grabs my hand and squeezes. Hard. "What happened?"

"Butter's a fainting goat. When she gets nervous, she freezes up and falls over," I say.

"That's the cutest thing ever," Theo coos.

Mercedes touches her hair. "I think I feel goat slime."

Theo grimaces. "But that's gross."

Mercedes punches him in the arm.

Addie scratches the sides of Butter's face. "She's such a sweetheart, and her vest is so cute!"

"Thanks, I made it just for her." I bend down and adjust Butter's vest so it sits a little straighter.

"What's going on in here?" Ms. Day asks, placing her bags on her desk.

Mercedes immediately launches into an explanation. "Addie, Theo, and I met early to go over audition details. As the play's director, I want to make sure I get an organized, early start."

Addie leans over and whispers in my ear, "Mercedes loves to get to school early. If she doesn't make up a reason for us to meet her, she ends up hanging out by herself, which she hates."

Mercedes crosses her arms. "I heard that, Addie."

"I wasn't trying to keep it from you," Addie says, laughing.

Theo plops into his chair dramatically. "It's so true."

"While that's great insight into Mercedes's character, I'm most curious about the goat." Ms. Day nods toward Butter, confused.

I'm ready with the certificate. I hand it to Ms. Day. "Butter's my emotional support animal."

Ms. Day inspects the certificate. "It says here she's a Tennessee fainting goat. That's an interesting choice for a comfort animal."

I nod. "We kind of found each other."

"That sounds fortuitous," Ms. Day says with a hint of amusement. "Let me just call down to the office and clear this with Principal Huxx." She walks toward the classroom phone.

My heart starts beating a million miles a minute. I don't want her to call Principal Huxx. "But Mr. J already approved it. He even wrote me a note," I say, turning Ms. Day's attention back to me. I hand her Mr. J's letter.

Ms. Day reads it. "Oh, I see." She gives the note back. "I didn't realize comfort pets were allowed at school, but it's my first year, so I'm still learning."

"ESAs are protected under federal law. That's what her tag says." I show Ms. Day Butter's tag.

Ms. Day's mouth twitches like she's trying not to smile. "Even so, I should probably call the office anyway. Just to check."

I pick Butter up and clutch her to me, suddenly

terrified we're going to get in trouble. I start to run through all the decisions that brought me to this moment, and my logic suddenly feels very faulty.

Ms. Day dials the classroom phone and . . . gets a busy signal.

Momentary relief washes over me as the bell rings and kids start to stream into the classroom.

Ms. Day hangs up the phone and comes back to us. "No one's answering, so I suppose Mr. J's note will have to do for now. Or until someone tells us something different. I wouldn't want to break federal law." Ms. Day winks at me and scratches Butter under the chin. "She really is quite adorable."

I snuggle Butter a little closer, feeling like we escaped an execution.

Kids begin to notice Butter, and they form a circle around us, asking a billion questions. It's like we're being swarmed by a hive of excited honeybees. They all want to pet her and know everything about her.

"Okay, folks. Take your seats and give them some space." Ms. Day puts her hand on my shoulder. "Marvel's emotional support animal will be joining us this morning."

I look back at Ms. Day and smile.

"You should probably go ahead and introduce your goat to the class and tell us about her because I can tell we won't be getting anything productive done until all their questions are answered." Ms. Day sounds bothered, but I can tell she doesn't really mind that Butter's presence is distracting everyone.

The entire class stares at us, and it is unnerving. This type of attention always makes my heart race, but running my fingers through Butter's wiry fur and focusing on Addie's encouraging smile calms my nerves. It's like throwing sand on a campfire. Underneath the coals smolder, but the flames are out.

I put Butter on the floor next to me. I take a deep breath and start. Everyone is quiet as mice while I talk.

"This is Butter," I say, my voice tight and higher-pitched than normal. I clear my throat and start again. "Butter's an emotional support animal. Her job is to help me feel more comfortable. She's special, though, because she is something called a fainting goat. When she gets stressed or anxious, her body reacts and she freezes up and falls over."

The entire class does a collective *ahh*. The volume in the classroom goes from sound booth quiet to concert level. It takes both me and Butter by surprise.

I hear Addie say, "Oh no."

Butter freezes and topples over. She rolls when she lands and ends up with her feet sticking up in the air.

The kids push back in their chairs and stand up. The scraping of the chairs and the kids' chatter are deafening. A voice breaks through the rest, Jamie's. "Classic!"

I look up to see Jamie recording Butter on his cell phone.

"That's enough," Ms. Day says. "Sit down, everyone, and be quiet. Jamie, hand over the phone."

"Whatever." Jamie hands Ms. Day his phone and mumbles, "If I act like a freak at school, can I start bringing my dog with me?"

Butter scrambles to her feet and looks around, unperturbed.

"Is she okay?" Ms. Day asks.

"Fine. Just startled." I give Butter a few encouraging scratches. "I think I'll hold her for a few minutes." I pick Butter up.

Her fainting episode starts another flurry of questions. The class wants to know where I found her, what she eats, where she sleeps, and every other question under the sun. Pretty soon, I forget I'm standing in front of the class, and I spend most of the period answering questions.

A few minutes before the bell is supposed to ring, Ms. Day says, "Before, when the class got noisy, Butter fell over. Can you give us some tips on how we can make her more comfortable in class?"

I go over some basics. "The more familiar Butter gets with her environment and the sounds at school, the more comfortable she'll get."

"Okay, class. I'm going to ask another question, but keep

in mind what Marvel just mentioned. We need to keep our noise level down, even if we get excited. Don't forget." She gives Jamie a pointed stare. Then she turns to me. "I know some working animals aren't allowed to be petted. Is that the case with Butter?"

"No. I'm okay if people want to pet her. She likes it."

As soon as I say this, kids hop up from their seats.

"Remember what we just talked about," Ms. Day says, and the whole class quiets again.

"Would you be okay if some of the more interested kids connect with you outside during our early-morning break to officially meet Butter?"

"Sure." I'm thrilled by our reception.

"I think we should let you and Butter head out first, then." Ms. Day gives Butter a goodbye pet.

Butter and I head outside. We hang out under a tree and wait for the bell to ring. There's a nice patch of grass, and Butter immediately starts nibbling on it.

Addie, Theo, and Mercedes are the first kids to find us. They run out the building doors and keep coming until they're a few feet away; then all three of them slow and approach Butter quietly.

Addie, Theo, and Mercedes spend the break with us. They pet Butter, police approaching students, and answer questions. Mercedes chats incessantly about the play. Theo cracks dad jokes (he must have a book at home or something), and Addie relays funny stories of our adventure to the pet store.

The entire time I'm at break, I don't think of anything at all. I feel like my mind is actually under the tree with the rest of me and not somewhere else running through an endless list of what-ifs. It's like a vacation from my brain.

When the bell rings to signal the end of break, I realize something—I'm really happy.

Then I see Principal Huxx striding toward us, her face pinched and livid. All my happy feelings fizzle.

I'm in big, big trouble.

BIG TROUBLE

Despite a gentle breeze, my skin burns like hot fire as I watch Principal Huxx approach, her body rigid with stern authority.

Addie looks from me to Principal Huxx, and her face scrunches with confusion. "She looks mad. Is this about Butter? I thought Mr. J gave you permission?"

I pick Butter up and hug her to my chest. "It was more implied than actual," I whisper, my voice shaky with dread.

Addie, Mercedes, and Theo exchange glances that say *Holy smokes* and *What was she thinking?*

My stomach churns, and I'm furious with myself for being foolish enough to think I could get away with bending the rules. I normally never break them or take risks because I can't bear the sinking distress and heart-pounding panic that's currently swallowing me up like quicksand.

Principal Huxx stops in front of us and wields her power. "You three, get to class. Marvel, follow me."

Addie, Theo, and Mercedes scatter with departing looks of pity.

Principal Huxx turns on her heel and heads toward the office. I don't move quickly enough, so she twists around. "Now, Marvel."

I jump up and follow her, my heart in my throat and my mind churning with all kinds of terrible fates—a huge fine I'll have to work off by spending extra time at school, automatic failure of sixth grade, or some other terrible thing Principal Huxx conjures up. I also vaguely wonder if I could go to jail for some reason. But the worst thought of all is of losing Butter because I think it might happen. Mom told me not to get attached.

I blink tears from my eyes and swallow down the rising nausea.

When we reach the office, Principal Huxx motions for me to go ahead of her but doesn't say anything. I almost wish she would. Her stony silence is way scarier than a freak-out.

Once we're inside, Principal Huxx says, "Enlighten me. Why did you bring a goat to school?"

I give Principal Huxx Butter's certificate and Mr. J's note with a shaking hand.

She inspects the documents while I bite my bottom lip waiting for her verdict. I silently repeat the phrase *protected by federal law* like a mantra, hoping it will save us.

Principal Huxx shakes her head, exasperated. "I must say, I'm at a complete loss how to handle this one. In all my years as a principal, no one has ever brought a goat to school before. Since Mr. J wrote the note, let's call him. Maybe he can explain it."

I gulp and buckle under the weight of my deception. I got Mr. J to write the note for a hypothetical support animal. Not a very real goat. "Do you have to call him? You have his note. I mean, I wouldn't want to bother him if he's busy." I shift Butter. She's getting heavy, but I'm afraid to set her down. I want to keep her as close to me as possible.

Principal Huxx squints at me like she's starting to understand what transpired. "I think we'd better. Don't you?" She picks up the phone and dials.

I want to tell her not to bother. That Mr. J doesn't know anything about it, but I'm very confused and frightened by her manner. She's not sounding mad, but she simmers like a volcano ready to explode.

Two seconds later, Mr. J comes into Principal Huxx's office. To his credit, he doesn't flip out. He only rubs his hand across his forehead as if he's trying to make his brain think. "Who's this?"

"Her name's Butter," I say, trying to be helpful.

Principal Huxx shoots me a look that says a million things, none of them kind. She hands Mr. J the certificate and his letter. "According to the document, this is Marvel's emotional support animal."

Mr. J stares at his note.

"I thought you might be able to shed some light on this situation since you seem to have agreed to it." Principal Huxx's tone is controlled, but her crossed arms and her stony face radiate anger.

"Give me a sec here." Mr. J looks truly flummoxed. I've never seen him flustered before.

Principal Huxx and I wait quietly for him to speak.

Butter, tired of being squished in my bear hug, wriggles free and jumps down. She eyes the note in Mr. J's hand and puts her front paws on his legs, trying to reach it. When she can't, she bleats in his face.

Mistaking her craving for paper with affection, he pets her. "She's friendly, huh?"

I pull her down. "Very."

"Why don't the three of us head to my . . . ?" Mr. J doesn't get to finish his sentence.

Principal Huxx finally gives in to her anger. She doesn't yell exactly, but the emphasis she puts on every word makes her mood crystal clear. "Absolutely not. No one is going anywhere until someone explains how Marvel got the impression I would allow a goat at school."

When she says it like that, then my plan does seem ridiculous. Worse, I think Mr. J's in trouble too and it's my fault.

"I can explain," I offer, trying to come to Mr. J's and my own defense. "An ESA can be any animal that brings their owner comfort. They're allowed into places pets usually aren't, like school, and it's okay because they're protected by federal law." I bend down and hold out Butter's tag as proof. I run my finger along the lettering and read it aloud in case they can't see it well enough. "Protected by federal law."

Principal Huxx stares at me like I've lost my marbles.

I let go of Butter's tag and slowly stand, afraid sudden movement might set Principal Huxx off.

She turns to Mr. J. "I think you better clear things up for Marvel while I get her parents on the phone."

Mr. J nods. "Marvel, go into my office, please. I'll join you in a second. I need a moment with Principal Huxx."

I go into Mr. J's office.

He takes more than a moment. I have about twenty minutes to agonize over what will happen when my parents arrive. Butter also has too much time on her hands and gets into everything. When Mr. J finally joins us, I'm pulling the edge of the beanbag out of her mouth.

He falls into his chair like he's had a very hard morning, which I suppose he has.

"Are you mad at me?"

"I'm disappointed."

That stings. Everyone knows that that's way worse than anger. Anger flares and fizzles out. Disappointment lingers. I look down at my hands, not wanting to meet his eyes. "I'm sorry for tricking you. I should have been up front from the start."

"I know you are. We can talk about it more later. Your parents are on their way, and before they get here, I'd like for you to tell me how you came by this unique support animal and why you think she would help you at school," Mr. J says.

I tell Mr. J about rescuing Butter, meeting Sonny the support dog, and how when I'm with Butter I feel calmer. "Goats are amazing creatures. There's a study that looks at goats and dogs. Apparently, goats are one of the only animals besides dogs to communicate with people through eye contact. They can be wonderful company, playful, and fun."

Mr. J pulls a folder filled with papers out of Butter's mouth.

I wince. I was too busy babbling about the benefits of goats to notice Butter tearing up his office. "Sorry."

He waves off my apology.

"They also make great support animals."

"How so?" he asks.

I'm a little unsure about this one. I wasn't able to find much information about goats specifically, so I wing it. "As you can see, they are friendly, funny, and trainable. You can train a goat to do anything a dog can do. Goats can heel and stay. They learn their names, come when called, and walk on a leash."

Butter knocks over Mr. J's trash can and starts munching on paper.

I right the waste bin and put the trash back into it. I wrestle a wad of paper from Butter's teeth and put her in my lap.

Butter wags her tail.

"She's precocious. I'll give her that." He pauses, and his face gets a little sad. "I do wish you had trusted me enough to be honest. If you had, I could have been clearer about the rules for emotional support animals and school."

I nod, feeling terrible.

"I think you misunderstood their access to public places. They are protected by federal law but only for specific and narrow purposes. A comfort animal isn't a trained service animal. So, while they're sometimes allowed to go places other pets aren't, they're not always guaranteed access. I'm sorry if I gave you the wrong idea." Mr. J is kind but firm.

I never imagined Butter's first day turning out like this. I thought if I presented all the paperwork, Principal Huxx and the teachers might be surprised or maybe annoyed, but they would have to let me keep Butter at school. Then I could go home and tell Mom and Dad I got permission to bring Butter with me. "I thought I knew what I was doing."

Someone knocks on the door, and I look up to see Dad.

I don't hesitate. I run to him and wrap my arms around him, tears streaming down my face. "I'm sorry. I know I didn't go about things in the right way. I just wanted to find a way to make school easier. It's gotten so hard, but I didn't want you to know how bad I was doing. I thought if I brought Butter with me . . ." I stop talking because I'm sobbing too hard to continue.

Dad kneels down to look me in the eyes. "I know how hard things can be for you. You don't have to hide it from me. I want to help you."

"But I didn't want to spoil your visit."

Dad holds my face in his hands and kisses my forehead. "This is life, Marvel. Not everything has to be perfect all the time and neither do you."

His words are such a relief that a fresh flood of tears falls from my eyes. I bury my head in his shoulder, and he rubs my back. I hang on to him, not wanting to let go.

Butter pushes her nose between Dad and me, making us both laugh a little bit.

Dad gives Butter a pat, then asks Mr. J, "Do you think we could talk privately?"

"Of course." Dad and Mr. J leave to talk while I wait with Butter. I pull her in my lap and hug her close, smushing my face into her fur, terrified I'm going to have to get rid of her after what I did.

After a few minutes, Mr. J and Dad come back with Principal Huxx. I know it's time to hear the consequences of my actions, and my heart thuds with dread.

Principal Huxx starts. "I'm incredibly disappointed in you. Bringing a goat to school is a flagrant disregard—"

Mr. J clears his throat, interrupting her.

Principal Huxx sighs. "Very well. I can't believe I'm going to say this, but Mr. J and your father have convinced me that you could benefit from a support animal and to allow your goat on a trial basis."

I sit up in my chair, confused by the new direction of the conversation. "What?"

"We know you're not the only child who suffers from anxiety. Mr. J thinks many of our students could benefit from having a comfort animal on campus, so he suggested we *temporarily*"—Principal Huxx peers down at me, making sure I hear the word *temporarily*—"allow your goat to come to school with you."

I can't believe what I'm hearing.

Mr. J continues. "Some of the other school principals

have already started allowing therapy dogs in their schools, and one school has allowed in a therapy pig."

"I heard about her," I say excitedly.

Dad shakes his head at me, and I realize the fragility of the situation. Principal Huxx agreed, but she's not convinced.

I close my mouth and let Mr. J do his thing.

"The school board is honoring principals who try out unique and innovative ways to help promote awareness for mental health. A goat as an emotional support animal is unique and innovative, so Principal Huxx has decided to give Butter a chance."

Principal Huxx holds up a finger. "But I have terms. First, the goat may not disrupt the school in any way. Second, she needs to pass an obedience test in one week. Mr. J will put together a list of skills we expect her to perform. Third, Marvel still needs to abide by the other parameters we set forth in the meeting—no absences, no late arrivals, no early exits, she completes any extra-credit work assigned to her by Ms. Day, and she performs in the play or else her promotion to seventh grade is in jeopardy. Are we agreed?"

Dad looks at me. "What do you think? This is your idea, so your decision."

I don't hesitate. "It's definitely a deal."

Principal Huxx holds her hand out.

I reach for it, and we shake.

"Your word is important. I expect you to keep it," Principal Huxx says.

"I will."

Butter bleats as if she also agrees.

Dad and Mr. J crack up. Principal Huxx's face doesn't move.

"I'll walk these two out," Dad says, and heads to the door.

Butter and I scramble after him.

I'm feeling so many emotions—disbelief, excitement, relief, love for Butter and Dad, gratitude to Mr. J and even Principal Huxx (which might be the most surprising feeling)—that I have trouble sifting through them all, so I don't. I roll them all up into one big ball of happy and let it bounce around inside me as Dad walks me and Butter to class.

Before I go into my classroom, he says, "Look, kiddo, I don't approve of the way you went about things. But I'm proud of you. A lot of navy cadets could learn something from you. You were smart, resourceful, and brave."

"You think *I was brave*?" I'm stunned he would say that about me.

He considers me for a moment. "You know, there are different kinds of bravery. Sometimes the hardest battles are in our own minds, and you fight those valiantly every day. That takes a special kind of courage."

I nod, disappointed, not feeling like that counts.

He playfully nudges me. "You also did well back there. That Principal Huxx is scary."

I try to wrap my head around his revelation. "Principal Huxx scared you? I didn't think anything did."

Dad pets Butter. "All kinds of things scare me. For instance, I have to go home and explain to your mother that I gave you permission to start bringing a goat to school. Now *that's* terrifying."

I laugh at him and nudge him back. "Mom's not that scary."

He raises his eyebrows at me and then smiles. "Maybe not. But when I am scared, I try to forge ahead anyway because a life lived in fear isn't much of a life."

I look down at Butter. "Yeah. I've been telling her the same thing."

Dad smiles at me and kisses my forehead. "I hope she's listening."

I hope she is too.

I gather Butter's leash into my hand, take a deep breath, and open the classroom door. For the first time in my life, I'm not worried about what comes next.

I'm ready for it.

DRAMA

Bayside Academy hallways are busier than Highway 101.
Kids zoom up and down in groups, talking, laughing, and
making plans to hang out. (Middle school is about social
connections, period. Only parents and teachers think it's
about learning.) Usually, I'm stuck navigating the halls
alone but not anymore. Now Butter accompanies me.

As we make our way to last period, she prances beside
me like she belongs. Even though the hallways are hectic,
Butter takes it in stride. I'm not sure if her easy comfort is
due to the fact that she's a herd animal, used to running
with a pack, so she thinks of the other kids as part of her
flock. Or if it's because the hallway noise hums continu-
ously in a predictable, monotonous din. It's loud, but there
are very few sudden, unexpected bangs to startle her.

Whatever the reason for her adaptability, she's acing it.

It's our second full day together, and it's exactly how I imagined it. Having Butter at school *does* help ease my worries. Taking care of her needs during the day keeps me out of my head and focused on the present. She's a living, breathing mindfulness exercise.

Butter and I head into language arts, which is the last period of the day because of my middle school's wonky, ever-changing schedule, and we go to our table.

Addie, Theo, and Mercedes are already there.

I sit down, and Butter puts her chin on the desk, expecting Cheerios. I give her a few. She gobbles them up and then wanders to Addie, Theo, and Mercedes in turn, greeting them.

"Did you get the list of skills Butter needs to perform from Mr. J?" Addie asks, giving Butter a vigorous scratch on her head, which causes Butter to close her eyes in bliss.

"Yep." I pull it from my binder and set it in the middle of the table so we can look at it.

Addie pulls it to her and reads. "Walk calmly on a leash." She looks up at me. "That's easy. She already does that."

I smile. "I know. Most of the others don't look too hard either, except for one."

Addie lists the rest of the skills. "Respond to her name,

come when called, demonstrate friendliness and adaptability, respond to the command *leave it*."

"Butter does most of those skills already, but I'm worried about the command *leave it*. Mr. J explained that one is about letting go of something I don't want her chewing on or doing, like butting people. Butter's proven herself to be a quick learner, but I have less than a week to teach her that." I start to fret about Butter failing her test. If Principal Huxx tempts her with paper, I'm not sure Butter will be able to resist. My anxiety kicks my imagination into gear, and I envision Principal Huxx cackling gleefully as Butter gobbles up reams of paper.

Just as I start to get stressed about how little time I have to train her and how much we have to accomplish, Butter sticks her head under my hand, insisting I pet her. I focus on her and stroke her soft ears, amazed by her spot-on intuition. It's almost like she has a sixth sense or something and knows when I need her.

Ms. Day calls our class to order. We're discussing the play again. My school takes the sixth-grade play very seriously. The students run the entire production: We pick which play we do, cast the show, figure out how to design the set, and run the tech (all the lighting). Ms. Day acts as an adviser only.

We already elected Mercedes to be the director, and today we're voting on which play to perform. Anyone interested in offering a suggestion goes to the front of the classroom to present their selection and give a few reasons for why they picked it.

I don't really care what play the class chooses as long as whichever one gets selected has a very, very, very small part for me.

Kiera and Kylie give their suggestion first. "We think our production should be . . ." Kiera and Kylie pause dramatically. Because of their names and because they look almost exactly alike, people always mistake them for twins. When that happens, they giggle and clasp hands as if they're two lost souls reunited at last.

"Yes?" Ms. Day prods. She doesn't seem annoyed, but she has to be. Apart, Kiera and Kylie are sweet. Together they're like a double scoop of chocolate chip ice cream—a little too much for one sitting.

"*High School Musical*!!" they scream in unison, jumping up and down.

"Good suggestion." Ms. Day writes *High School Musical* on the board.

A few more kids go, and the list grows long.

Hamilton. (Does anyone sing and dance?)

Peter Pan. (Where will we get a crocodile?)

The Giver. (Too sad.)

Sleeping Beauty. (Only if it's a feminist retelling.)

Romeo and Juliet. (Shakespeare and romance, ugh.)

A Midsummer Night's Dream. (We're not British.)

I can tell Ms. Day is partial to the Shakespeare recommendations, but before she can close out the suggestions for voting, Mercedes and Addie pop their hands into the air.

"Okay. Last one. Come on up," Ms. Day says.

Addie and Mercedes stand.

On their way to the front of the room, Mercedes grabs Theo by the collar and says, "All three of us came up with this idea."

"Yeah, but I don't think Marvel's going to like it," Theo mumbles, and gives me an apologetic grimace.

I immediately perk up. What do I have to do with it?

The three of them get situated at the front of the room. Addie gets the ball rolling. "This year, we have a unique opportunity to do something special and include ALL the members of our class."

"Yep, that's right. *All* the members of our class." Mercedes practically radiates with pride at her own soon-to-be-revealed genius, and I get an uneasy feeling. I can't figure out how I'm involved in their plot. I'm only participating in the play in order to pass sixth grade. I have no plans to do more than the bare minimum required for that single goal.

"Soooo..." Addie draws out her vowels for effect. (There actually has been a lot of drama during these

suggestions. You'd think we could save it for the performance.) "We think we should do a play called *Heidi*."

I relax a little. I'm unfamiliar with their suggestion, but
it sounds harmless.

"Never heard of it," Jamie calls out. "Sounds boring."

"Jamie, we discussed safe space rules," Ms. Day says,
but I don't know why she bothers. He never listens to
anything.

Mercedes takes over. "It's a story about a girl who goes
to live with her grumpy goat-herder grandfather in the
Swiss Alps. Because the story is set in a small cabin in the
mountains, the set will be super easy—"

Addie interrupts Mercedes just as I'm mulling over goat
herder and trying without success to connect the dots.
"And most importantly, we have our very own goat!"
Addie points to Butter.

The classroom erupts in excited chatter.

Butter stops eating Cheerios and looks around as if she
knows everyone is talking about her.

I stare at them, horrified by their suggestion. I try to get
their attention by bulging my eyes out at them and shaking my head no vehemently, but all three of them ignore
me on purpose.

"Creative!" Ms. Day says and writes *Heidi* on the board.
"Time to vote."

Good grief.

Ms. Day passes out little pieces of paper and tells us to jot down our first choice.

Kiera and Kylie are asked to collect votes. It's like having twin ushers on either side of the room. I have to give Ms. Day credit. It's truly efficient. They make short work of the collecting, and Ms. Day tells us to do some group work while she counts the votes.

Addie, Mercedes, and Theo use the downtime to talk.

Butter, sensing an opportunity to demand attention, sticks her nose toward Addie for petting. Addie obliges her, stroking between her eyes and then scratching the side of her cheek.

"So . . . what do you think of our brilliance?" Mercedes asks, proud of herself.

Her idea is bonkers, not brilliant. "Butter can't be in a play. The sounds of the theater will scare her. She'll spend the entire performance fainting."

"If she can come to school, she can be in a play," Mercedes says firmly. "Besides, I've got a whole protocol figured out."

I'm skeptical, and I've got an awesome eyebrow raise. I use it.

"For real, I've got it all planned out. She'll be fine. Don't worry," Mercedes says.

That's like telling me not to breathe.

"And the winner is . . ." Ms. Day says, and the whole

class immediately gets quiet and focuses on her. "*Heidi*! It looks like Butter has made quite an impression on everyone."

Mercedes beams as if she's won the lottery. "Yes!"

Theo and Addie give each other high fives.

"Aw, come on!" Jamie bellows.

The whole class starts chattering, excited about the show. No one has even asked me if I'll let Butter do it.

I get lost in my thoughts, thinking about how I'm going to get Butter out of this mess. I try to figure out a way I can break the news that there's no way Butter can perform in the show. I mean, she has issues with noise and she's not even fully trained yet. How will she be part of a play?

All of a sudden, I hear Mercedes say, "Marvel will be perfect!"

"Huh?" I say, coming back to the present.

"You're going to play Peter, the supporting lead. He's a goat herder and in all the Swiss Alps scenes, so it's perfect. With you playing Peter, Butter's handler will always be on the stage with her. See, I've got it all figured out."

I'm positively gobsmacked. Mercedes has completely lost her mind. I couldn't even do a ninety-second speech without freezing. How am I supposed to play a supporting lead? I'm not doing it. No way, no how, and I tell Mercedes exactly that. "You saw my Famous Californian speech. You know I can't be trusted. I'll ruin the whole performance. I'm not doing it and neither is Butter."

"We'll see," Mercedes says, and buries her head in her homework, becoming uncharacteristically studious and silent.

Terror makes my heart thump wildly against my chest as visions of her wacky plan coming to fruition unfurl in my mind. Between my freezing and Butter's fainting, the play will be utter mayhem and I'll fail sixth grade for sure.

"Mercedes," I hiss, trying to get her to look at me so we can agree her ridiculous idea is absurd and impossible.

Mercedes puts a finger to her lips and shushes me. "Ms. Day is speaking."

I glare at her, appalled. That's never stopped her from talking before. I cast glances at Addie and Theo, trying to enlist their help. Both quickly dip their heads down and stare at their notebooks, suddenly as conscientious as Mercedes.

My exasperated sigh is intentionally loud as I gather Butter in my arms and cuddle her, trying to calm my rising panic. The play can't hinge on us. We'll never survive the ordeal, and the play will be a complete disaster.

I have to make Mercedes see reason.

I sneak a peek at her. The determined scrunch creasing her forehead as she pretends to read her notes makes one thing crystal clear—changing her mind will be a battle.

LEAVE IT

The face-to-face battle I expect to have with Mercedes never comes. Instead, she sends in a stealth attack.

After school, Addie walks home with me and Butter. Most afternoons, Addie has activities—dance, swimming, music, tutoring—if there's a class offered, Addie takes it. Some days, she's even double-booked, so I know this is a setup.

It's not like I don't feel guilty. I want to be the kind of kid who can perform a lead role with ease, and I know Mercedes has her heart set on having Butter in the play. She dreams of being a real director when she grows up and thinks that if her directorial debut features a live animal, it will make her college applications stand out. *College applications.* Mercedes's determination and laser focus on the future give me heart palpitations. While she's plotting a life course intent on world domination, I'm simply hoping to pass sixth grade.

Regardless, I'd love to help her achieve her goals, but I can't. Even with Butter at my side, performing a supporting lead in the play is simply too much to hope for from me. Mercedes has to understand that.

When Addie and I get to the middle of the field, I unhook Butter's leash. She pretty much follows me everywhere I go now, so I like to give her some freedom and let her run. As soon as I do it, Butter bounces away a few feet before turning around and coming back to me.

Addie watches Butter, amazed by her obedience. "My dogs don't behave that well off-leash. To be honest, they don't behave well on-leash either. They're pretty much fur monsters."

I laugh. "Fur monsters."

Butter runs up to us and lowers her head like she's going to butt us.

"Leave it," I say, using a stern voice.

Butter stops for a second, and I think she's going to listen. Then she rams her head into Addie's leg.

"Hey! Talk about fur monsters." Addie laughs and rubs her shin.

I put Butter's leash back on. "Did she hurt you?"

"No, she's too small." Addie reaches over and pets Butter. "You little devil."

"She can't do that during her obedience test," I say, stressed about how much depends on Butter passing that test. If she doesn't, Principal Huxx won't allow her to come to school with me anymore. School is so much better with Butter that I can't imagine going back to what it was like before.

"It's not until next week, right?"

I nod.

"You'll get her sorted out." It occurs to me that Addie is an optimist, always looking on the bright side. I really like that about her.

We stop to let Butter nibble on the grass.

"About the play," Addie says, bringing up the subject I knew was coming.

"Addie, you saw what happened to me when I did my Famous Californian presentation. I was a disaster. I had stage fright so badly, I literally froze in front of everyone. Jamie's right. I *am* Frosty."

"True." Addie pokes me in the side with her elbow and smiles. "The good news is you can't get any worse."

"Addie . . ."

"I'm only joking. But Butter will need you onstage. If you play Peter, you'll be with her in all the scenes."

I make Butter start walking again. If she had her way,

we'd stand there all day while she munched on grass. "But who says I'm letting Butter do it?"

"The whole class voted for her. You have to let her be in it. Plus, Mercedes is counting on Butter to draw big crowds and make our play the best one the school has ever produced."

I groan. The idea of big crowds only makes me more nervous.

I don't say anything else for the rest of the walk. When we get to my house, I linger at the garden gate feeling torn. I really don't want to disappoint my new friends, but they don't understand what they're asking of me. "I'm really sorry. I know Mercedes has her heart set on it, but we can't do it."

Dad comes from behind the gardening shed carrying a huge bag of mulch and asks, "Can't do what?"

I give Addie a *don't share what we were talking about* look. She either can't read social cues or is choosing to ignore me because she says, "For Butter to be in the school play."

I wonder if I know Addie well enough yet to stomp on her foot.

Dad sets down his bag of mulch. "They've asked Butter to be in the play? How did that come about?"

Addie jumps in to answer before I have a chance to respond. "We took a vote on the play we're going to perform, and we all picked *Heidi* because of Butter. It was unanimous."

It totally wasn't. Two people voted for *High School Musical* (Kiera and Kylie) and one person voted for *Hamilton* (me). I mean, it's an awesome musical, and there are a lot of crowd scenes where I could be onstage but hide behind everyone else. And I know Jamie didn't vote for *Heidi*.

Dad moseys up to the fence like he's settling in for a long chat. "Wow! The kids must really enjoy having Butter at school. Ms. Day was on board with that?"

"All for it," Addie says. It's like Dad and Addie are besties. "But Marvel's not sure."

"Why not?" Has he completely forgotten about my stage fright?

"The *incident*," I say. "And it might be stressful for Butter."

Dad puts on his solemn navy face and glances at Butter. "That goat's a trouper. She's proven she can adapt. I wouldn't worry about her. As for you, I think you can do anything you put your mind to."

Does no one get it? My mind is always the problem, not the solution.

"That's what I told her! Mercedes, our director, has a foolproof plan to make sure Butter is completely comfortable. Besides, we know we'll draw a huge crowd and sell lots of tickets if Butter is in the play. Most of the money goes to charity too, so it's for a good cause." Addie should be a salesperson when she grows up.

"I'm happy to help with the set if you need volunteers," Dad says, surprising me. He doesn't have a ton of time for his leave, and I have no idea why he would want to spend a chunk of it building scenery for a middle school production.

"We definitely need someone to help with that. Another reason for you to do it, Marvel." I can tell Addie feels very proud of herself by her smug smile.

"When does practice start?" Dad asks.

"In a few days. Mercedes is still casting the other parts."

"I'll let you two finish your negotiation. But if you want my two cents, I think you should do it." Dad hoists the bag of mulch over his shoulder again and heads toward the front of the house.

When he's out of sight, I ask, "Why do you think he offered to build the set?"

"Probably because he wants to spend time with you. That's why my mom volunteers so much," Addie says.

Hmm. That never occurred to me.

"Did I convince you?" Addie crosses her fingers and bounces on her toes like a little kid begging for a new toy.

I'm 100 percent positive I'm still a hard no. I can't play Peter. I'm going to struggle enough with a small part, but I'm unsure about Butter after Dad's comments. Butter *might* enjoy it. She loves being around the kids at school. The play would give her more time to interact with them, and I do have confidence in Mercedes's abilities to create a welcoming environment for Butter. I'd also love to spend more time with Dad.

"What's the charity?" I ask.

"We plan to donate to an animal organization in Butter's honor," Addie says, tugging at my heartstrings.

I look down at my toes, feeling horrible about disappointing everyone and wishing I was the kind of person who took risks.

"The whole class is counting on you. They voted for you and Butter," Addie says.

"They voted for Butter." I bite on my lip, thinking. Most likely, no one really cares about my participation, except for Principal Huxx, and I have that worked out. If I can train Butter to follow someone else's commands, then they won't need me.

Addie smiles. She thinks I'm going to crack.

She doesn't know who she's dealing with. I'm a pro at manipulating technicalities. I have to be. Otherwise, I'd never survive my anxiety. "Have Mercedes cast Theo as Peter, and I'll train him to work with Butter."

"But it's your part."

"I don't want it. I'm supposed to get a small one. Something tiny." I hold two of my fingers a millimeter apart and show them to Addie so she knows exactly what I mean by tiny. "Give the role to Theo. I'll teach him to work with Butter. It's a win-win for everyone. Trust me, no one wants the play to hinge on me."

She sighs, "If it gets Butter onstage, I think Mercedes will agree."

"Pinkie promise," I say, and hold out my little pinkie.

"Pinkie promise."

Addie and I latch fingers, and the deal is sealed. Relief washes over me, and the tension in my shoulders that I didn't even realize I was holding eases.

When she leaves, I decide to work with Butter on the obedience skills Mr. J gave me.

I feel confident she knows her name, but I spend some time checking to make sure. I sit in her enclosure with her and call her name repeatedly at random intervals. Whenever I say it, she looks up and stares at me with her ice-blue eyes. She's definitely got that down.

I decide to work on something harder, the command *leave it*. I'm not exactly sure how to teach it to her, but figure the best way to practice is to let her wander around the garden since there's lots of stuff in it she shouldn't touch. I'm not concerned about her getting into real trouble because I plan to stay nearby to keep her out of it.

I unclip Butter's leash, walk a few feet away, and wait to see what she does.

She eyes me coyly, then starts to explore the garden. For the first fifteen minutes, she wanders around interested but respectful, checking out the plants like she's on a horticultural tour. (These are very boring. Trust me. I've been on several with Mom.)

That's why I don't think much of it when she sniffs one of Mom's roses and pushes a large, impressive bloom with her nose.

I get close to her and use a calm, authoritative voice as I say, "Leave it."

Butter pauses and looks at me with her gentle eyes before chomping the head off the rose.

Oops.

I'm bending down to pop Butter's leash back on when Mom's voice booms across the garden. "Marvel Madison McKenna!"

The yell startles Butter mid-chew and she topples over.

I'm not sure who to attend to first, Mom or Butter. I look between them and decide that since I'm closest to Butter, the best thing I can do is get her leash back on.

Mom makes her way across the garden to us. "What in the world are you doing?"

"Teaching Butter the command *leave it*," I say.

"It doesn't look like it's working," Mom observes with unnecessary snark.

199

"We just started. She can't be expected to know how to do it yet."

Mom inspects the gnawed stem and shakes her head. "My garden isn't the place to teach her that. I don't know what's gotten into you lately. Put Butter in her enclosure, and come inside for dinner."

I take Butter to her enclosure and then go inside.

It's not a pleasant family dinner. Mom made pasta, which is tasty, but impossible to enjoy because Mom aggressively spears ravioli with her fork like she's still mad at me.

Halfway through our awkward meal, Mom's phone buzzes on the kitchen counter, and she stands to get it.

"Don't we have a rule about media at the table?" Reef asks, seizing the opportunity to pull his cell phone out of his pocket and start scrolling.

"This family has no discipline," Dad says, clearly resigned to our slovenly ways. We are the polar opposite of military order.

"Reef, put your phone away. NOW," Mom growls. "I'm expecting a call about a new landscaping job. Being available when you are the sole member of your own company is not the same as scrolling through social media."

"Yeah, Reef," I say, backing Mom. She rarely misses an opportunity to school Reef on any number of life lessons, and I find these moments very entertaining. Plus, I'm trying to get back on her good side.

Reef glares at me and slides his phone into his pocket.

Mom reaches for hers and looks at the screen. "Huh," she says, sounding confused.

"Who is it?" Dad asks.

"Not sure. The number's unfamiliar. I better answer it just in case." Mom slides her thumb across the screen. "Hello?"

Mom stops talking while she listens to the caller on the other end of the line. Then she says, "You're calling from the zoo?" Mom pauses and then says, "I think there must be a misunderstanding. We haven't found a capybara. Although, I must confess, I'm not even sure what that is."

Dad, Reef, and I look at one another, perplexed.

"Oh my," Mom says. "We definitely do not have a hundred-pound water rodent in our backyard . . . Yes, I'm very sure. Okay, bye." Mom drops her phone on the dining table next to her place setting and shivers, creeped out. "I didn't know such a thing existed."

"What was that all about?" Dad asks.

Mom glowers at me. "I'm not sure. Maybe your daughter can explain why someone at the zoo saw her posting on Nextdoor and thinks she found a gigantic rodent and brought it home?" Her voice rises in intensity as she talks.

I grimace, thinking about the fuzzy picture I posted. Based on the doctored photo and the vague description that made Butter sound more like a monster than a missing goat, I suppose someone could have mistaken Butter for a capybara. I shrug. "No idea. People on Nextdoor are weird." I grab my plate and try to stand up from the table.

Mom puts her hand on top of mine. "Not so fast. When was the last time you checked Nextdoor to see if anyone has responded to your posting about Butter? She has an owner, and I want you to be prepared if she shows up. You've gotten really attached." She gives Dad a pointed look when she says this like he let it happen.

"Um . . . recently?" I stand up, more than ready to skedaddle.

"Hold it. Pull up the posting." Mom hands me her phone.

My mouth goes completely dry. My plan for Nextdoor depended on Mom *not* checking it. "Okay."

I hand the phone back to Mom.

Mom's face goes from white to red, back to white again. She's furious. She thrusts the phone at Dad. "Look at what your daughter wrote."

I can tell he wants to be mad, but when he sees the picture, he has to work hard not to laugh.

Mom scowls at Dad and then swivels around to lecture me. "There's not a single piece of useful information in this listing. If you don't even try to find her owner, it's like stealing. You can't take someone's pet."

"But they're not a good owner and they don't deserve

to have a goat as amazing as Butter. Butter *needs* me. Look how good she's doing and look how good I'm doing. I'm WALKING to school. I'm making actual friends."

"Honey, I know. We're so proud of all the progress you've made. We know Butter is a big part of that. But sometimes, I wonder if you're really dealing with your anxiety. It's great that Butter helps you feel braver and calmer, but do you really have control over it? Are you practicing any of the skills Mr. J taught you?"

I stand up from the table. This time Mom doesn't stop me. I scrape my plate into the compost. Mom is adamant about composting. It's her gardener's obsession. I shove my plate in the dishwasher. "I don't need any of that stuff anymore. I'm doing great."

Mom gives me a look that says a gazillion things. *I'm worried about you. Are you sure you're as okay as you think? Be more realistic.* She might as well add, *Do your homework*, her look says so much.

I shrug her off. She doesn't understand. Everything is all better now. Butter fixed it. There's nothing to worry about anymore.

Mom starts typing on her phone. "I'm changing the Nextdoor posting. If Butter was meant to be yours, then she will be. Honestly."

Butter is already mine. That's what Mom doesn't understand.

21

SHE FOLLOWED ME TO SCHOOL

By the end of our first week of going to school together, Butter and I fall into an easy, happy routine.

Each morning, I wake up eager to start the day and rush to get ready. Then I race outside to see Butter. No matter how early I get to her enclosure, she's always thrilled to see me and greets me with cheerful bleats. I make sure to take care of her needs before mine and give her fresh water and hay before going back into the kitchen to grab my own breakfast, which I bring outside to eat with her.

When it's time to leave for school, we walk across the soccer field together. I've become so accustomed to the field that I almost can't remember why I used to be afraid of it. I suppose humans have the same ability to acclimate to their environments as goats.

Butter loves our walks. She runs, jumps, and plays the whole way like nothing in the world matters except making me laugh at her antics and the joys directly in front of her.

This morning, Butter decides to explore a new part of the field and darts to the edge, where she pauses at a patch of thistles growing alongside it. Mom would be appalled if she saw the weeds growing unchecked and I'd be terrified that one of the prickly barbs might get stuck in my skin, but Butter has none of those concerns. She sticks her nose right into the cluster of flowers and sniffs curiously.

One of the thorns jabs her sensitive pink nose, and she hastily jumps back in alarm, vaulting herself into the air. She does a half-body twist like a surprised cat and lands on all four hooves. Then she shakes her head, frantically trying to remove the spike.

I laugh, my love and adoration for her welling up in my heart and overflowing like a waterfall. I'm not sure I've ever been so perfectly happy before.

"Silly goat," I say, and rescue her by removing the thorn before releasing her to play some more. She trots off to continue exploring her surroundings in a seize-the-day-type way.

Watching her makes me wish I could be exactly like her and take each moment as it comes instead of constantly agonizing over what might happen next.

As the school gets closer, so do my worries. Mom meddling with the Nextdoor posting means there's a greater risk that Butter's old (horrendous and terrible) owner might actually see it and show up to claim her, but I shove that thought far away. The idea of losing Butter is so unbearable, I can't think about it for a single second.

A more immediate concern is Butter's upcoming test with Principal Huxx. We're almost at the end of our trial period. Butter's made some progress with the *leave it* command, but not enough that her response to it is dependable. If she fails the test, our days of going to school together are over.

Then there's Mercedes. She hasn't shared the casting list with anyone yet, even Addie. It's possible that she won't honor Addie's pinkie promise to give me a small part in the play instead of assigning me Peter. Ms. Day assured me a small, nonspeaking part would meet Principal Huxx's requirements as long as I had multiple appearances onstage, but she doesn't cast the play—Mercedes does. So I'm at her mercy and every time I try to bring it up with her, she changes the subject. Mercedes has big plans for the play that include Butter, which by default involves me.

Butter and I make our way to language arts, where we'll learn our fates for the play. When I get to my table, I take a seat and lean toward Addie to whisper in her ear, "Did you convince Mercedes to agree to our deal?"

She gives me a noncommittal shrug that doesn't instill a lot of confidence. "I talked to her. She wasn't happy about it."

I grimace, feeling unease grip my stomach and twist it like a hand wringing out a sponge. I contemplate appealing to Ms. Day if Mercedes insists on casting me as Peter, but I doubt it will do any good. The whole goal of the play is to empower the students to produce a totally kid-run production. Ms. Day acts as our adviser only, and she doesn't interfere.

Ms. Day turns the class over to Mercedes so she can unveil the cast list. Mercedes is like a demigod holding my fate in her hands. I really hope she's a benevolent one.

Turns out she's a long-winded one. Mercedes goes on and on about her vision for the play, the practice schedule (every day after school for the next four weeks), call times the day of the play, and blah, blah, blah. She talks so long, even Butter gets lulled into dozing off.

About five minutes before the end of class, Ms. Day gently prods Mercedes to hurry up. "Mercedes, I don't mean to interrupt. Your attention to detail is commendable. You're definitely the right person for this job, but if you don't get to the cast list, you're going to run out of time."

Mercedes looks up at the clock. "Right!" She hastily

pulls out a notebook and grandly gives out roles. "Addie will play Heidi."

Jamie interrupts her. "Aw, man, this whole thing is rigged. That's total nepotism."

"It's only nepotism if we're related, you . . ." I think Mercedes is going to call Jamie a name, but she checks herself at the last minute. "Addie has the most experience and gave the best audition."

Ms. Day doesn't comment but goes to Jamie's desk and casually stands by it in a total teacher move to restore order.

Theo gives Addie a high five.

I whisper congratulations to her, but I have no idea why she's excited. It sounds like a death sentence to me.

Mercedes glares at Jamie and says, "Grandfather will be played by Jamie."

"That's what I'm talkin' about!" Jamie shouts.

I roll my eyes as my confidence in Mercedes's decision-making falters.

"Aunt Dete will be played by Kylie," Mercedes says with a note of apology in her voice.

Kylie's typically placid demeanor sags with unhappiness. "She's the villain."

"I know it wasn't your dream role, but I had to do it because of casting restraints." Mercedes gives me a pointed, disappointed look and quickly adds, "Peter will be played by Theo."

Theo looks down at his hands, upset, and I wonder why. It's a huge role, and he'll get to work with Butter.

Addie rubs his back and whispers something in his ear as I bite my bottom lip, wondering what's going on. I want to ask them, but don't have time because the bell rings.

As people get up to rush out the door, Mercedes says, "The rest of you will be townspeople and crew."

Theo bolts out of the classroom before I can talk to him, so I grab Addie by the arm. "Is Theo okay?"

"He'll be fine. He had his heart set on playing Aunt Dete, that's all."

"Oh," I say as guilt squirms around my stomach like a worm. "Why?"

Addie shrugs. "He says she's the villain and has all the best lines."

It never occurred to me that Theo might not want to be Peter. "Will you tell him I said thanks?"

"Of course, but don't worry about it. We all want Butter in the play, and this is the way that's going to happen. He'll be fine." Addie's kind voice absolves me, but that makes me feel worse.

Addie smiles at me. "I'm going to try and catch up to Theo. See you later in social studies?"

I nod and watch her go before gathering my things.

Ms. Day spots me and says, "Can I speak to you for a minute?"

"Sure." Butter's nap infused her with energy, so I let go of her leash to let her wander and she's bouncing around the room. I wonder if I'm in trouble for letting her roam freely.

Instead of chastising me, Ms. Day says, "I have a proposition for you and Butter."

I'm immediately relieved but grab Butter's leash anyway and pull her close to me. "Really? What?"

She smiles at me and Butter. "Some of the teachers were talking and wondered if you and Butter might be willing to visit the lower school next week?" At our school, the lower school means a couple of different things. It's physically lower. It is on the same campus but down a flight of steps. It also means the younger grades. My school is K–8, so we're all in one big jumble, but they like to keep us separated by levels.

"Sure. Why?"

"We thought it might be nice if you two spent time down there. Some of the younger kids struggle with separation anxiety, and a comfort animal might be just the thing to take their minds off it. If you also write a personal narrative about your experience, it would give you an opportunity to earn some of the extra credit you need for me. I thought doing something you enjoyed would take a bit of the sting out of the extra work." She hands me a thick packet. "This is the makeup work from your other teachers. If you could return it on the Friday before the play, you'll be all caught up."

I appraise the bulging packet and sigh. By the weight, it feels like a ton of work. I stuff it in my backpack and focus on the more pleasant part of our conversation. "Butter and I would love to visit the kindergartners."

"I thought you would." Ms. Day pets Butter on the head. Butter responds to the affection by butting her on the leg in an attempt to get her to play. Ms. Day rubs her shin but smiles. "How *are* the two of you doing on the list Mr. J gave you?"

"Great," I say, trying not to think about Butter's inconsistency with the *leave it* command.

Ms. Day smiles. "That's excellent because the other reason for your visit to the lower school is Butter's obedience test. Principal Huxx plans to observe Butter there. Mr. J and I thought it might be a more relaxed, natural environment for both you and Butter."

I gulp. That sounds completely alarming. She might have led with it.

Ms. Day gazes at me with kind concern. "Butter's been doing well in class, I'm sure she'll continue to impress."

I nod and turn to leave.

Wanting to prove Ms. Day's word true, I encourage Butter to prance along beside me by holding her leash taut and rewarding her with Cheerios when she falls into step next to me. After we walk a few feet, I glance up to see if Ms. Day is watching us.

She gives me two thumbs-ups.

When we reach the door, Ms. Day says, "Oh! One more thing. You should ask a friend to join you for your visit to the lower school. You might need help with crowd control."

"Crowd control?"

Ms. Day laughs. "You're visiting the kindergartners after all. You're likely to get mobbed."

Fantastic, a test and a mob.

I stare at Ms. Day, hoping she might have some more advice, but she's turned her focus to something on her desk, leaving me to stew over the upcoming visit without any additional guidance or words of comfort.

I pull Ms. Day's door closed behind me and try to shut out my rising anxiety. Butter and I have to pass that test. If we don't, my days at school will return to the way they used to be—stressful, sad, and lonely, and I can't let that happen. Ever again.

TEST

All weekend, the lower school visit and Butter's test loom over me. Butter and I spend Saturday and Sunday practicing. By the end of the weekend, she understands all the skills perfectly, except for *leave it*. That one trips her up, especially when I tempt her with paper.

On Monday morning, I get Butter ready for school with a deep pit in my stomach and trembling hands. Even the sweet smell of her hay and the reassurance of her fur as I stroke her can't quite soothe my jagged nerves. There's too much at stake.

Butter has only come to school with me for one blissful week, but my life has changed drastically for the better. I have three friends instead of none, a plan for surviving the cursed play, and a companion who helps me cope with my anxiety when it tears at my insides like a piranha.

If Principal Huxx bans Butter from school because we fail the obedience test, my world will revert to the way things were before Butter, and I can't go back. Not now. I've gotten a glimpse of what life can be like without anxiety clouding every emotion, every decision, every thought, and it is so much better—freer, lighter, happier. I want to keep moving forward, out of the fog. Not turn around and lose myself in it again.

We *have* to pass that test.

Butter and I walk across the field quickly without making our usual stops for her to play and frolic, which might be a mistake since a tired goat is a well-behaved one, but I don't want to be late.

We make it to school in record time and head straight to the playground, where I arranged to meet Addie. Ms. Day told me to bring a friend, and Addie, with her easy-going personality, was a natural choice. Though, I would have been happy to have Mercedes or Theo with me too.

When Addie sees me, she waves with her usual cheer. "Ready for the scary kindergartners?"

I twist the end of Butter's leash in my hand. "I'm prepared for them. It's Principal Huxx who frightens me."

Addie grins at my dramatic reply. "You and Butter have got this. Don't worry!"

Telling me not to worry never works, but her faith in us does help a little.

We make our way down the steps into the kindergarten area. It's a pretty section of the school, comprising a large green lawn with a big oak tree and five classrooms.

We arrive before any of the students, but Principal Huxx is already there waiting for us. She clutches a clipboard in one hand and a pen in the other. For some reason, the clipboard freaks me out. I know it's an inanimate object, but it somehow manages to be judgmental anyway.

"Prepared for the test, Marvel?" Principal Huxx says, clicking her pen.

Dread seizes my stomach, making me feel nauseous. "We've been practicing a lot," I say, sounding as nervous as I feel.

"They're going to ace it." Addie's unfeigned enthusiasm causes a wave of gratitude for her to wash over me.

"We'll see." Principal Huxx peers down at me like a raptor, and I wonder if she purposely tries to resemble a vicious predator or if her demeanor is accidental. "During the visit, I'll be watching Butter. By the end of it, she must demonstrate friendliness and adaptability, respond to the command Mr. J gave you, and walk on a leash."

My rising tension at the task ahead and my need to check one item off the list makes me blurt out, "But she already walks on her leash like a pro."

Principal Huxx pauses for a moment. "I must admit, I do see she's mastered that skill."

I wonder if the disappointment I hear in her voice is imagined or real. Before I have time to think about it, the kindergartners start to arrive, and Principal Huxx moves to the side of the lawn to observe us.

The first kids to come down the steps are two boys with identical features. They barrel our way, swinging lunch boxes at each other like battering rams.

Addie's eyebrows shoot up, astonished by their unruly behavior. "I hope they're not all like that."

"I think they might be," I say, feeling panic-stricken. Directly behind the twins, an oncoming horde of little kids charges toward us at top speed. I point them out to Addie.

She grabs my arm. "It's like a Viking invasion."

The atypical alarm in her voice spurs me into action. I scoop Butter up and drag Addie with me as I duck behind the oak tree to hide us from the marauding kindergartners while we come up with a plan to keep from getting mobbed.

I peek out from behind the tree. "None of those kids look like they have any issues with separation anxiety."

Addie leans around me to get a look. "Not those kids. They seem a little *too comfortable* at school if you ask me."

I poke my head around the tree again and see Principal Huxx scribbling on her clipboard. That can't be good. Hiding behind a tree is the opposite of adaptability. I have to find a way to salvage this situation fast. We need to get out there, but I don't want Butter to get scared and faint before she has a chance to show what she can do.

"What's the plan?" Addie asks without taking her eyes off the wild kids.

I bite my bottom lip and force my brain to think. I see a nice spot on the lawn away from the chaos, and I get an idea. "Maybe if I sneak over there and sit down with Butter on my lap and the kids come over in pairs, it won't be too much for Butter."

"Sounds like a plan. But how are you going to get there without them seeing Butter and going gaga over her?"

"Do you think you could create a distraction while we get settled?"

Addie considers this. "Probably. Our neighbor has five little kids, so I have experience distracting little terrors. I'll cover you while you get settled."

"Thanks, Addie."

"Anything for Butter," she says, and then bravely runs into the throng of kids, yelling, "I'm a scary monster! Catch me!"

Every single one of the kindergartners chases after her. She runs in the opposite direction, leading the kids away. I use the distraction to carry Butter over to the patch of grass and sit down, cradling her in my lap.

I notice Principal Huxx jot something on her clipboard. I wonder if Butter's being adaptable enough or if the need to give her a calm environment to meet the kids is a mark against her.

When Addie puts enough distance between her and the majority of the kids chasing her, she stops running and whispers into the ears of two little ones fast enough to stay on her heels. Then she points in our direction. As soon as they see Butter, their eyes light up and they bolt toward us.

I motion for them to slow down and be quiet. To my complete surprise, they do. When they reach me, I pat the grass on either side of me. "Sit here and here."

They settle next to me and cross their legs.

The little girl has long, dark hair tied into two pigtails and wears a multicolored dress and rainbow tights, mixing every color in the spectrum in a creative but cute way. "Can I hold your goat?"

I answer as kindly as possible because away from the crowd of other kids, she no longer looks like an attacking Viking, but a sweet, chubby cherub. "Once Butter gets used to you. She's a fainting goat. When she gets scared, she stiffens up and falls over, so we want to make sure she's comfortable first."

The little girl nods, shaking her pigtails as if that makes complete sense to her.

The little boy holds his small hand out toward Butter and then hesitates. With an adorable lisp, he asks, "Am I allowed to pet her?"

I start to give my permission, but Butter beats me to it and pushes her nose under his outstretched hand. All three of us laugh.

I look over at Principal Huxx, hoping she saw the exchange because making little kids happy has got to earn points, but her eyes are focused on the clipboard instead of us, so I'm not sure she noticed.

Addie continues to send kids over in pairs until there's a huge group of kindergartners sitting in a circle with me and Butter. Then Addie joins us, finding a spot across from me.

My anxiety drives me to keep checking Principal Huxx's responses to see if Butter is passing the test or not, but there are too many kids for me to pay attention to them and her. I force myself to stop looking in her direction and focus on the kids.

Before I know it, I'm having such a good time telling the little kids everything I know about goats, I *almost* forget Principal Huxx is watching me.

Butter wriggles free of my lap, and I let her go. She wanders from kid to kid, accepting gentle caresses and the occasional kiss good-naturedly, as if she knows her job is to charm and delight them.

When the bell rings, all the little kids reluctantly say goodbye to Butter.

Addie comes over and gives me a high five. "That started out rough, but ended up pretty good, huh?"

"I think so," I say, and finally allow myself to glance at Principal Huxx. She's still writing on her clipboard but looks less like a raptor than she did at the start of the test. I desperately want to find out the results of her assessment, but don't want to do anything to mess it up now because I think it went well. "Do you think we should just go or stay?"

Addie shrugs. "Probably get going. Always leave them wanting more, as they say in show business."

I shake my head and laugh at her. She's got a good point, but I don't know if I can leave without a verdict. I'm still debating what to do when a little girl in a red dress and her mom enter the kindergarten area.

The girl's dark hair is snarled with tangles like she just woke up and her long lashes glint with tears.

They pause outside a classroom door, and the mom kneels down to talk to her daughter. From their conversation and the way the girl clings to her mom's shirt, it's clear she doesn't want to go into her classroom. I know how she feels.

"I'm going over there," I tell Addie.

Addie nods. "She does look like she needs cheering up, but are you sure you want to hang around longer than you have to? I think the test went great. Maybe you shouldn't push it."

Addie has a point. I look from Principal Huxx to the little girl, feeling torn. I want to be done with this whole ordeal, but I know I can't leave without trying to make the girl feel better.

"I have to try to help."

Addie nods. "I get that."

Butter, Addie, and I walk toward the mom and daughter. When we get close to them, Addie hangs back and I approach them with Butter. "Would it be okay if your daughter feeds my goat a treat?"

The little girl's mom looks at me like I've just thrown her a life preserver. "Ellie, would you like to feed the cute goat?"

Ellie sniffles and nods.

I put a Cheerio in Ellie's hand and show her how to hold it flat with the food in the center of her palm. Ellie extends her hand out to Butter, and she sucks up the Cheerio like a vacuum cleaner. Ellie giggles, delighted, and her mom mouths *thank you* to me.

I bend down and drape an arm over Butter's neck. "My other favorite thing to do is take Butter for a walk. Would you like to try that?"

Ellie looks at her mom for permission. Her mom nods, and Ellie says, "Yes, please."

I hand Ellie Butter's leash, and she walks Butter around the lawn as Addie drops Cheerios on the ground in front of them to keep Butter moving.

We take a couple turns around the circle and then steer them back to the classroom door. Ellie returns the leash to me but still doesn't seem to want to go into her classroom.

"Did you know Butter goes to school here?" I ask.

Ellie shakes her head.

"She does." I point in the direction of the upper school. "Addie, Butter, and I are in sixth grade."

"Do you think you can be brave like Butter and go to school today?" I ask Ellie.

Ellie pauses for a moment, then gives a noncommittal shrug. I try to keep from smiling, feeling a kinship with her. Like me, she's not going to be easily tricked into doing something she doesn't want to do. I totally get her.

I offer something a little more enticing. "How about if we promise to visit you at lunchtime? Then do you think you could go to school today?"

Ellie vigorously nods her head.

Her mom smiles at me as if I'm an angel from heaven and quickly drapes a backpack on the little girl's slight shoulders. Ellie turns to go inside, and I notice that her backpack is unzipped with a single piece of paper hanging out of the top.

Butter notices the paper at the exact moment I do, and the leash goes taunt in my hand as Butter starts to lunge for it.

Three things happen at once. Principal Huxx's watchful eyes snap up from her clipboard to stare in our direction. Addie puts her hand over her mouth in horror. I command Butter to *leave it* with more authority than ever before.

Butter pauses mid-lunge and looks at me for a single second, but it's enough. Ellie slips into her classroom, and the tempting paper disappears with her.

Butter bleats at me, annoyed by her lost opportunity, but I ignore her and shoot my eyes toward Addie to share a knowing look full of relief.

Ellie's mom, completely unaware of the narrowly averted disaster, says, "Wow. That was amazing. Wait until I tell all the other parents about this. I don't know how to thank you girls and your goat enough."

I shrug with a nonchalance I don't feel. My heart still races from the close call with the paper. "It's okay. I know what it feels like to not want to go to school. Butter makes it better for me too."

"You two girls and Butter are amazing." She gives Addie and me hugs.

Principal Huxx comes over. When Ellie's mom sees

her, she reaches out to embrace her too but pulls up when she notices Principal Huxx stiffen. They end up falling into an awkward handshake-hug combo.

Despite the weirdness, Ellie's mom gushes her praise. "This school is amazing. Thank you for being a creative and innovative leader."

Principal Huxx looks taken aback at the glowing compliment. "You're welcome."

"I'm going to get out of here while I can, but I'll tell everyone I know how wonderful you are, Principal Huxx," Ellie's mom says before leaving.

Principal Huxx turns toward me, rips a piece of paper off her clipboard, and hands it to me. "Give that to Mr. J."

I look down at the paper and see *PASSED* scrawled across it in capital letters and Principal Huxx's signature at the bottom along with a lot more writing, but I don't care about the rest. Only the one word matters to me. "Thanks."

"Don't thank me. You earned that."

There's a hint of irritation in her voice that I don't know how to interpret. I can't tell if she's upset that Butter passed her test or bothered by something else, but at the moment, I don't care. Butter can keep coming to school with me, and that's all that matters.

Principal Huxx leaves, and Addie and I wait in excited silence until she's out of sight. As soon as she's gone, we jump up and down in celebration. After we've bounced ourselves out, we gather our things and practically skip to class, giddy with success.

When we walk in, Ms. Day greets us. "How did it go?"

Addie pets the top of Butter's head. "Great! You should have seen Marvel and Butter. They were amazing with those little kids."

"Well done! I didn't expect anything less," Ms. Day says, smiling.

At her words, my chest puffs up and feels like it's going to burst. The sensation takes me by surprise because it's not one I'm familiar with. For a second, I think I'm having a heart attack. Then I realize it for what it is—pride.

I DO NOT WORK WITH ANIMALS

Mercedes is a wonder kid. She knows all these acting terms like *on your mark*, *stage left*, *stage right*, *blocking* (where to stand when, kind of like stage choreography), ASM (assistant stage manager), and *doofer* (a word for any tool she doesn't know the name for and that she uses constantly). She carries a book called *On Directing* tucked under her arm and reads it whenever she has a spare moment. She even halts rehearsal to reference it about a trillion times each practice.

We've already had five days of play practice, and Butter loves it. She likes the way all the kids (except for Jamie) lavish her with attention, but I'm not sure she has a future as an animal actor. She's not the most flexible thespian. She loves to work with me, just not anyone else.

I hold Butter on her leash in the wings, and Theo stands next to me as we wait for our cue. We're working on an emotional scene where Heidi reunites with her grandpa after time away. Since Grandpa is a goat herder, Mercedes wants Butter to be onstage during the scene.

"To give the illusion of being in the Swiss Alps," Mercedes says grandly.

Right now, I walk Butter out on her leash, but our goal is to train her to follow Theo without it. Theo's very sweet to Butter. She'll be in good hands with him. Only, Butter doesn't want to be in Theo's hands. She wants to be in mine.

"Okay, everyone on their marks. Grandpa? Heidi? Goat? Peter?" During rehearsal, Mercedes only calls people by their character names. She thinks using our real names will cause us to suddenly remember we're kids, not the characters in the play.

"Action." Mercedes doesn't yell this. She has given strict instructions that everyone is to talk in normal voice levels out of consideration for Butter's sensitivities, and I adore her for it. She's incredibly committed to Butter's contribution to the play, but I wish she wasn't so excited about it. That way, we could just forget the whole thing.

I put my hand on Butter's head and stroke her, letting the motion calm me. Practicing hasn't been too bad.

Mercedes has been coaching me. She tells me to forget Marvel and focus on Butter. When I'm more focused on Butter and what she's doing than on myself, it makes everything easier. Of course, I don't actually plan on being the one up there opening night. That will be Theo, so practice is okay because there's no real pressure.

I have a townsperson part like I wanted, and all it requires of me is to blend into the crowd whenever Heidi and her grandpa come off their mountain for a visit.

I hand the leash to Theo. "You walk out with her this time so she can get used to you."

"No problem." Theo takes the leash and feeds Butter a Cheerio.

Butter, Theo, and I walk onto the stage.

Mercedes gives us an approving head nod.

"Okay, let's add something," Mercedes says. "Goat? Trainer? Peter? A word." Mercedes talks completely differently when she's directing than when she's just her normal self.

Theo and I lead Butter toward the edge of the stage and crouch down.

Mercedes whispers, "How's that kissing trick coming?"

"She's almost got it." After we passed the obedience test, I started working with Butter on an adorable trick. I'm training her to stand up on her hind legs and touch her nose to my cheek like she's giving me a kiss. Unfortunately,

I made the mistake of showing it to Mercedes, and now she's obsessed with working it into the play.

"Good. I'd like to add it into the end of this scene. I think it would add a little something extra if Butter jumped up and kissed Grandpa."

I look at Jamie. "Maybe you should clear that with him first?" Jamie is SUPER into acting (who knew?) and hates working with Butter.

"Nope. I want to get a cold reaction. That way I'll know what his surprised face should look like." Mercedes is into method acting, which means she wants everything to be authentic. Unfortunately, her method often proves painful for her actors. "What's the cue for that?"

"I touch Butter on the tip of her nose, and when she gives a kiss, I reward her with a Cheerio."

"That's perfect! Show it to Theo." Mercedes gives Butter a scratch behind the ears. "You're going to make this show epic. No one has ever had a live animal in a student show before."

I pat Butter and think of all the things that could go wrong. But I've been trying to master my worry and go with the flow.

Theo and I head to a quiet part of the stage, and I teach him the command. "Think you've got it?"

Theo nods. "Yes, but don't you think it would be easier if you just played Peter? He doesn't say much. He mostly

229

wanders around and calls to the goats. It's boring. Personally, I'd rather be Aunt Dete. She's the villain and has the best lines."

He's been saying this same thing to me about a hundred times a practice, but I don't think he's looking at it the right way. "But you get to be with Butter. She's essentially the star. Mercedes planned the whole play around her."

"Exactly! I don't want to be upstaged by a goat!" Theo says.

"Theo! Seriously?" I laugh. I can't even begin to relate to him. All I want to do is hide behind Butter.

"Places, people. We're starting the scene from the top," Mercedes says.

Theo, Butter, and I go back to the stage wings and wait for our cue. "Marvel, let Theo take this one."

"This is a cold run. Butter hasn't practiced it before. Are you sure that's a good idea?" Theo calls to Mercedes.

"Yep, all good. Let's go, people," Mercedes says.

I'm not sure it's a good idea either, but I hand Theo the leash.

When the cue comes, Theo and Butter walk out.

Jamie sits on what is supposed to be a boulder, but it's really a stool created to look like a rock thanks to some theater-set magic. When Theo and Butter get to him, he scowls. Since grumpiness is part of Grandfather's character, it's hard to tell if he's acting or hating on Butter.

Jamie says his lines.

Addie says hers.

Jamie says his next line.

Then it's time for Butter's new trick.

Theo gives her a light tap on the tip of her nose and points to Jamie.

She jumps up and puts her hooves on his chest.

Jamie FREAKS OUT. "Ugh . . . get it off me!!"

Startled, Butter jumps back, freezes up, and falls over. Her legs stick straight out.

Jamie throws down his cane, rips off his wig, and stomps off the stage, yelling, "I DO NOT WORK WITH ANIMALS."

Mercedes pole-vaults onto the stage. "Oh no. Butter. I'm so sorry."

I run out to Butter and reach her just as she scrambles to her feet.

Mercedes takes Butter's face in her hands and attempts to examine her. "I didn't think he'd react that way. Do you think she's okay?"

Butter pulls away from Mercedes and trots to my side. She seems more annoyed by Mercedes's inspection than Jamie's outburst. I bend down and put an arm around her. "She'll be okay."

Mercedes looks into the curtain wings where Jamie stands pouting. "That's good. I should probably go deal with Jamie." She walks away, muttering something about actors that I can't quite hear.

Theo rubs Butter's nose. "I'm sorry, Butter."

"It's not your fault. You did everything right. It's him." I glare at Jamie.

Theo looks at Jamie too, only his expression is wistful. "Maybe I should have *that* role. It's a meaty part, and I'd get to be creative with the makeup to make myself look like an old man."

"But what would Butter do without you?" I ask in an attempt to keep Theo interested in the role I need him to play.

"Turn to you, her person," Theo says, trying to hand me the leash.

I push the leash back toward him. "You just need to spend more time with her. She adores you."

"Maybe." Theo's apathetic tone makes me nervous, and I decide he really does need to spend some one-on-one time with Butter to get psyched up about being her handler.

"Watch Butter for me, okay?" Before he can argue, I shove the leash at him and walk away through the backstage area and out the door.

I don't have anywhere to go, but I want to him give him time alone with Butter so they can bond. I stand outside the door for about fifteen minutes, giving Butter and

Theo a heavy dose of quality time. Maybe if I do this every practice, they'll be good buddies by opening night.

When I get back, Mercedes marches toward me, looking really annoyed. "We need to talk. *Privately.*"

Maybe I was gone too long.

She takes my arm and pulls me aside. "I need you to play Peter."

I'm stunned by her unexpected pronouncement, and my stomach rolls with fright. "What? Why?"

"Butter. She's not going to work for anyone else, and she's harassing everyone. Look at her."

I thought Butter and Theo were bonding. I search the auditorium for her. She's not with him. Instead, she's roaming around nibbling on anything and everything, including people's hair and their scripts. It's surprising how comfortable she's gotten with the kids in such a short period of time.

"Sorry, I thought Theo had her. He needs to be more invested in her if he's going to be her onstage handler. You should probably talk to him."

"That's part of the problem. Theo really wants a better part, and I want to give him one. He's been looking forward to this play all year. It's not fair to make him stand in for you because you're afraid."

I glance over at him. He's staring at Mercedes and me. When he sees me looking at him, he quickly turns his head.

"Look, I get it," Mercedes says, drawing my attention back to her. "Stage fright is real. All the best actors experience it."

Out of nowhere, my eyes sting with tears. Hearing Mercedes acknowledge my stage fright instead of telling me it's all in my head, and making it seem normal instead of freakish, is so caring and accepting that it bowls me over.

Mercedes takes both my hands in hers. "If you do this, you'll have me as your director and Butter onstage with you the entire time. You'll have each other. What do you think?"

"Maybe Theo just needs a bit more time to adjust to the idea?" I sneak a peek at him.

"He really doesn't want to do it. If you agree to this, he can be Aunt Dete. You know he's dying to play the villain. But the only way he can is if you agree since Peter and Aunt Dete are onstage at the same time. And Kylie would love to get out of playing Aunt Dete. She hates the idea of being the meanie. You'd make them both happy."

I pause, thinking.

"Besides, even though Peter is onstage quite a bit, he only occasionally yells Heidi's name. You can *totally* handle it," Mercedes says.

I don't want Theo or Kylie to miss out on their chance to have the role they want because of me, but

Mercedes is asking too much. I shake my head. "I can't."

"Please. All of us believe in you and will help you every step of the way. You also have Butter." Her brown eyes beg me to change my mind, and I really want to make her and the rest of the kids happy.

I bite my bottom lip, considering her words. Even though I've been petrified I'll freeze up again, things *are* different now. When I did my Famous Californian presentation, I didn't have Butter, Dad home, or friends. Everything has changed since Butter came into my life. And I've changed. With her by my side, I'm different. Maybe the play will be different too. Before I fully realize what I'm saying, the words slip out of my mouth. "I'll do it."

"Great!" Mercedes hugs me.

Theo joins us. "She agreed?"

"She did," Mercedes says.

Theo throws his arms around me too, mushing us into a three-person hug.

"What's going on over here?" Addie asks.

"Marvel agreed to be Peter!" Theo says.

"Wow. About time." Addie nudges me. "Wait until Jamie finds out. He's going to have a major temper tantrum."

Mercedes rolls her eyes. "Don't even get me started."

Theo hugs me again. "Thanks, Marvel."

I smile. "Sure. But if I can't get the words out on opening night, it will be up to Addie to wing it and cover for me."

"No problem. I got your back." Addie gives me a fist bump.

"All right. Enough of this," Mercedes says, getting back to business. "We have work to do. Peter. Heidi. Go work with the goat. Aunt Dete. You have lines to memorize and blocking to learn."

"Yes," Theo says, and victory-punches.

After play practice, Addie catches up with me. "Mind if I walk home with you?"

"Not at all!"

"I can't believe Jamie scared Butter. Do you think she'll do the kissing trick again?"

I stroke her ears. "Eventually. She's a smart girl, and she doesn't seem to let stuff faze her." I could take a lesson or two from her.

Addie strokes Butter's other ear. "I'm really glad you decided to play Peter. We'll get to be in a ton of scenes together, and it will be super fun."

I nod and start to regret my hasty decision. Hanging out with Addie will be fun, but the idea that I have to be in a ton of scenes makes me queasy.

We get to my house, and Addie stops at the fence. "Would you help me run lines tomorrow before school?"

"Sure." I open the gate and walk through. "I'd love to."

Addie hangs over the fence to give Butter some extra pets, and Butter jumps up to get closer to her.

"Thanks for walking home with us."

"I like hanging out with you," Addie says.

I'm surprised by her response. Addie has so many other friends. "I like hanging out with you too."

Butter bleats at Addie, and I laugh. "I think that means she also likes you."

"Well, that's good because I like her. See you in the morning." Addie waves and heads home.

As I watch her go, I realize I have something I've always wanted. A best friend.

24

CONNECTIONS

During play practice, I help Addie run lines away from the main group, which is awesome. I'm reading Peter. He really doesn't have too many lines. He only has one scene where he says something other than Heidi's name, but it's still a huge amount of pressure.

"You're really good, Marvel," Addie says. "I keep forgetting it's you talking and not Peter."

"Thanks." I'm surprised at how much I like rehearsing. It's easier being Peter, the character, than it is being me. When I'm reading lines, it's like putting on a mask and Peter's nothing like me. He's brave and outgoing and doesn't let anything worry him. The only thing Peter and I have in common is our love of goats.

I'm having so much fun with Addie, I'm starting

to think I might possibly be able to manage this new role. The weirder part is how much I want to try it. I'd love to show Dad what I can do before he has to leave again. I only wish I could get over the waves of nausea that overtake me every time I think about actually doing the show instead of just practicing for it.

Addie rolls the script up in her hands and pretends to be the mean grandfather. She delivers a line and fumbles it badly.

I try not to laugh, but I can't help it.

Addie starts to crack up.

It's not even that funny, but we can't stop laughing.

Mercedes spots us goofing off and hurries over. She runs a VERY tight ship. She puts her hands on her hips and scowls. "What's going on over here?"

This makes me and Addie laugh harder.

"What's so funny?" Mercedes asks.

We can't even stop long enough to answer her.

"Get it together, you two, and get onstage. I'm ready to do our first run-through of the scene where Heidi visits Peter at his home."

That stops me laughing.

Addie and I take our places. The set for the scene is simple—a table and two rocking chairs, and I only have one major line. When Peter's grandmother asks how his reading is going, Peter says, "Just the same." It shouldn't be hard, but somehow it is.

"Places, everyone," Mercedes says.

Addie sits at the table across from Jada, a kind girl Mercedes casted as the grandmother. I settle into one of the rocking chairs and hold Butter's leash loosely to give her enough room to move a little.

Mercedes scans the stage with her hands on her hips. We all know that stance by now. It's means something isn't to her liking. She considers the set for about five minutes and finally says, "I don't think a goat would be inside the house."

"But I thought Butter was supposed to be in all the scenes with Peter?" I say, reminding Mercedes of our deal.

"But it doesn't look right. Let's try it a few times without her. It's just rehearsal." Before I can complain, Mercedes leaps up onto the stage and leads Butter away.

I watch Butter go, feeling panicky.

"From the top," Mercedes says.

Addie runs through her lines, and then Jada says hers. They go back and forth a few times, and then it's my turn.

I whisper, "Just the name."

Mercedes says, "Marvel, your line is *Just the same*. Not *name*, and speak louder, please. Project. From the top, everyone."

We start again. When it's time for my line, I try to do

what Mercedes wants and speak up, but I overcorrect. I get the line right, but the volume of my voice is so loud it echoes around the auditorium.

Everyone watching snickers, and I see Jamie doubled over, laughing hysterically in the stage wings.

My face turns bright red.

"Don't worry, Marvel. You'll get it," Mercedes says.

Unfortunately, her prediction never comes true. Every time we run the scene, I mess up. When I don't improve after multiple attempts, Mercedes finally decides to work on something else.

Grateful to be free, I dart offstage, collect Butter from Mercedes, and look for a place to hide for the rest of practice. I find a quiet spot backstage, and I'm there feeding Butter Cheerios when Dad shows up with a wooden cutout of a mountain. He's been building a mountain range out of plywood to mimic the Swiss Alps. He's been coming to school at the end of practice every day to deliver more pieces of the set and then walks home with me.

Dad leans the mountain against the wall and brushes his hands off. "Hey, kiddo. What are you doing back here?"

"Hiding."

He smiles and sits down next to me. "And why are you doing that?"

"Because I kept messing up our scene." I sound petulant.

"Hmm. First time you ran through it?"

"Yeah. How did you know?"

"An educated guess. Nothing ever works right without practice. You'll get it." His calm confidence makes me want to believe him.

"Do you really think so? Because I'm worried I'm going to be a disaster."

"I really think so," he says, and puts his arm around me, pulling me close. "And even if you don't, everything will be okay."

Somehow the strength of his arm around me makes his words feel solid and trustworthy, so I let myself believe them. We still have a few weeks of practice left. Maybe if I can convince Mercedes to let Butter be in the scene with me, I'll be able to do it.

Butter jumps up and puts her front hooves on Dad's stomach. He scratches the sides of her face as he would a dog's. "Are you ready for dinner?"

"She's eaten half the play scripts already," I say.

Dad chuckles. "She's a goat. It's in her nature, but maybe we should feed her something with more substance and you need dinner too. What do you say we go home and forget about plays for a few hours?"

"That sounds great," I say, and we head out the stage door.

Outside, the temperature has dropped and the fog is starting to roll in. That's one of the crazy things about the

Bay Area. It's warm and sunny one minute, and cold and foggy the next. It's something about the way the city is in between the sea and the mountains.

"You know, I remember one night on the ship when the fog was so thick, I couldn't even see my hand in front of my face. There were no stars, and if it weren't for our instruments, we would have had no idea where we were going," Dad says.

I imagine it and get a familiar sick feeling in my stomach. I don't like when Dad talks about his time at sea. I hate thinking about him being out on his ship away from us, and I really don't want him to talk about going away again.

"You know I'm going to be heading out to sea again."

I unhook Butter's leash so she can run. "Do we have to talk about that? I don't want to think about it."

Dad takes my hand. "Marvel, we can't ignore the hard stuff."

"Why not?" He might not be able to, but I can. I have him home, I have friends, I have Butter. For the first time in a long time, life feels pretty good. I'm not going to muck it up by thinking about hard stuff.

"Because, kiddo, the hard stuff has a way of catching up with us whether we want it to or not."

I choose not. "So, you think Butter has bad manners, huh?" I ask, changing the subject.

Dad sighs. After a few seconds, he says, "I think she has terrible manners."

I laugh and swing our hands as we walk. "Me too."

Dad chuckles, and life is perfect. Me, Dad, and Butter all together.

LAST STRAW

I'm on the playground before school with Butter. It's my favorite place to train her because there are so many things for her to climb on. She still hasn't mastered bowing or jumping up on a surface on command and I need her to do both for the play, so we're here to practice. I still have a lot of conflicting feelings about the play. One minute I'm super excited about it. The next I'm wishing I could hide under a box until it's all over.

I take Butter over to a bench that sits on the edge of the playground. I manage to coax her onto it and reward her. She's so clever and picks up tricks quickly.

Ms. Day sees us and comes over. "Well done! Butter is going to be amazing in the play."

I smile. "I think so too."

"I hear you're doing a pretty good job too. I'm proud of you. You've come a long way these past few weeks, and you're going onstage as Peter!" Ms. Day pats me on the shoulder.

"Thanks."

"I'm glad I found you out here. I was wondering if you and Butter would be interested in making a last-minute appearance in the third-grade classrooms this morning? Their state assessments are today, and we think Butter could really help with the nerves."

"Sure!" After our success with the lower school visit, I'm eager to do it.

I head down to the third-grade wing and wait outside the classrooms for the bell. Our job is to visit each class for a few minutes to spread peace and calm. Almost all the kids know Butter by now, so this should be easy-peasy, and the truth is, I am feeling proud as a peacock to be entrusted with this job. Butter and I are doing something special and making a difference.

The first visits go smoothly. All the third graders really appreciate having Butter visit them, and we're almost done. Just one class left.

I open the door to the last classroom.

I have Butter do a few of her best tricks for the kids— she kisses, high-fives, and stands on her hind legs. The third graders love it.

My favorite way to end a visit is to let the kids feed Butter Cheerios so they can feel her muzzle tickling their palms. It's always a hit.

I hand out Cheerios and the kids laugh when she eats them out of her hand, and that's it. That's all we have to do.

I'm getting ready to leave when Ms. Stewart stops me. "Do you think you could help me move some of these desks around for the test before you go?"

"I'd be happy to." The desks are grouped for collaborative work, not the best formation for testing.

I let Butter's leash go and tell her to stay. She gives me a pouty look. I pet her head. "You'll be fine! It'll just take a second."

Ms. Stewart and I get to work moving the desks around. There are thirty of them. Every few minutes, I look over to make sure Butter is where I left her.

"Two more," Ms. Stewart says.

"Great." I help her move one.

"How do you get your goat to do all those tricks? I didn't know goats could do that." Ms. Stewart adjusts the desk we moved to line it up with the others.

"It's not as hard as you think. Goats are really—"

"Ms. Stewart." A third grader comes up and taps her on the arm.

"Hold on, Annie. Marvel is telling me something.

Remember, we talked about waiting for your turn."
Ms. Stewart turns to me. "Go on."

"Well, goats are really smart. They can do almost anything a dog can. Do you know they were one of the first—"

"Ms. Stewart." Annie taps her again.

"Annie, I'll be right with you, sweetheart. Marvel was talking, and she's our guest. She gets to speak first, and we let her talk until she finishes."

"Okay," Annie says.

"They were one of the first domesticated animals."

"Wow. That's interesting."

Speaking of animals, I haven't checked on Butter for a few minutes. I turn my head and look for her.

Butter is still standing where I left her, but she has somehow pulled a box of papers off Ms. Stewart's desk and onto the floor. They're strewn all over the place, blanketing the floor.

Butter stands in the middle of the mess, happily munching on the papers like hay.

Ms. Stewart gasps and puts her hand over her mouth. "Oh no!"

Annie pokes Ms. Stewart again. "That's what I was trying to tell you!"

I run over to Butter and take the papers away from her and try to put them back in the box, but there are too many sheets to clean up quickly and several are shredded, multiplying the mess. I'm still on my hands and knees trying to clean up when I say, "I'm sorry. I should have been watching her. Were they important?"

"Very. These papers are the state tests." She looks stricken as she pulls the trash can over. She starts gathering up handfuls of the documents and dumping them in the trash, but the mess is overwhelming and she leans back on her heels as if defeated by the task.

I keep cleaning as she stands up and goes to the classroom phone.

A sense of growing doom makes my chest constrict. "Are you calling someone?"

Her kind face turns grave as she says, "Principal Huxx. There are very strict state rules about the tests. I have to let her know right away."

My heart sinks. Eating state tests definitely falls under the category of being a public nuisance. Butter's never going to be allowed to come to school with me again.

It takes about two minutes for Principal Huxx to get to the classroom.

She takes one look at the eaten tests and shakes her head in dismay. "Follow me to the office. We need to call your father to come pick up the goat. Innovative or not, I can't allow her at school after this."

My head hangs low and tears fall from my eyes as Butter and I follow Principal Huxx to the office.

GRANDMA PRISBREY

For the first time in three weeks, I go to school without Butter, and it's like a piece of my soul is missing. The whole day, I count the hours and then minutes until I can see her again.

Thankfully Butter is still allowed to be in the play. When the bell rings, Addie and Mercedes walk home with me to pick her up for play practice.

Mercedes chatters the whole way, talking about stage makeup tips she picked up from a ballerina on YouTube. While Mercedes talks, Addie playfully dances around Mercedes and me, making us giggle. I love hanging out with both of them and think I might like to try ballet class again if the play goes well.

When my house comes into view, Mercedes pauses

mid-sentence and puts a hand on Addie to keep her from twirling. "Do you have company staying with you?"

"No. Why?"

Mercedes points to a white pickup truck with a trailer parked in my driveway.

"Huh." I don't know anyone who drives a truck like that. Probably one of my mom's landscaper friends.

Addie's stomach rumbles. "I'm starving."

"Me too. Let's check on Butter before I grab snacks." I walk through the back gate and into the garden. As soon as I get close enough and see the top of Butter's head, I breathe a sigh of relief to be near her again. I peek over the enclosure fence and see her nibbling happily on hay.

She senses me, and pops her head up. She chews peacefully while watching me with her ice-blue eyes.

I lean over the fence and pet the side of her face.

Addie, Mercedes, and I go into the enclosure, and smother her with love.

I snap her leash on her collar and hold the leash out to them. "Do you mind hanging with Butter while I run inside to get our snacks?"

"Yeah, we'd rather not," Mercedes teases, and I laugh because I know they love Butter almost as much as I do.

Addie takes the leash, and Mercedes grabs Butter's brush. "We'll fancy her up. I can't have my star performer going around ungroomed."

Butter bleats as if she's skeptical of Mercedes's definition of fancy.

I smile at Butter and kiss her pink nose before departing.

"Mom!" I call as I walk inside. "Whose truck is that in the driveway?"

"It's mine," a woman's voice says from the living room.

I pause mid-step and turn.

An older woman with gray hair is sitting on my couch. "You must be Marvel. Your mother's been telling me about you." The baggy sweater and loose-fitting blue jeans she's wearing look oddly similar to my Grandma Prisbrey costume. It's almost as if she took it out of my closet and put it on.

"Yes. Who are you?"

The older woman stands up. "My name is Gloria Fizzle. I'm thrilled to meet you. Your mom has told me how you cared for my sweet Butter. I don't know how to thank you enough."

"What are you talking—"

Mom comes into the living room, interrupting me. "Marvel, this is Gloria . . ." She pauses, uncomfortable. "Butter's owner."

"But I'm Butter's—

"Honey, she saw the posting on Nextdoor," Mom says, her voice a mixture of guilt and regret.

I shake my head. I can't be hearing Mom right.

Mom wraps her arms around me. "She's come to claim Butter. She's been searching for her."

"*No*," I snap. "Absolutely not." This is outrageous. Who does this *Gloria* think she is? She can't waltz into my home and take Butter.

Gloria looks remorseful. "I'm so sorry, dear."

I push away from Mom. "How do we know this woman isn't some imposter? The Internet's full of dangerous scammers. Where's the proof she's Butter's owner?" I twist my hands, frantic for a solution because Mom acts like she's going to hand Butter right over.

Gloria shows me some documents. "These are Butter's registration papers. I've been raising mini myotonics, a special breed of fainting goats, for about thirty years."

For someone who has been raising goats for so long, she's not very good at it. This woman lost Butter. Those papers don't mean anything. She isn't a fit caretaker for Butter. "You abandoned her! Left her to fend for herself. When I found her, she was being teased by a group of kids. She was all alone and terrified. She was eating garbage out of a trash can!" The volume of my voice shocks me, but I can't help it. My fear, anger, and heartbreak pour out of me in a waterfall of uncontrollable emotions. She can't take Butter. She just can't.

"Marvel! That's enough," Mom says, appalled by my

behavior. "This is Butter's owner. She has every right to claim her."

Gloria looks miserable. "I discovered a hole in the fencing around her pasture. I have no idea how she made it all the way over to your school. I searched everywhere for her. I've kept looking for her this entire time, but I feared the worst. I'm so thankful you found her and protected her. I hate to think about what would have happened if you hadn't saved her."

Gloria tries to put her hand on my arm. I jerk it away.

The front door opens, and a few seconds later, Dad stands next to me, taking in the scene. Relief washes over me like a wave. Now that he's here, he'll fix it. Ever since Butter came into my life, he's been our ally. He loves Butter as much as I do. I slip my hand into his. "She's trying to take Butter. Tell her she can't."

Mom quickly fills Dad in on the situation.

As she talks, his trustworthy, always-straight shoulders droop. "I'm sorry, sweetheart."

My brow creases with confusion. "Tell her she's not allowed to take her."

He answers with stoic heartbreak. "You know I can't."

My heart fills with a dread so heavy I feel like I'm sinking. I squeeze Dad's hand tighter. "Please," I plead. "I need her."

Gloria gives me a sad smile. "I didn't mean to upset anyone. I should probably get Butter and head home."

"Of course. I'll take you to her." Mom leads Gloria toward the back door and the garden.

"Dad, no! Don't let them." I try to run after Mom and Gloria.

Dad catches me by the waist. "Marvel, you can't."

"She's taking Butter!" I break free from him and run after them.

Addie and Mercedes stand inside the enclosure and watch, confused, as Gloria takes Butter. As soon as they see my face, they seem to understand.

Dad catches up to me and holds me in place while Gloria leads Butter away.

Mom wipes her eyes. "I'll walk you around to the driveway."

Butter hesitates and looks back at me, bleating.

Gloria gently coaxes Butter forward, but she digs in with her back hooves, refusing to be led away.

Gloria glances in my direction, and I think she's going to change her mind. Instead, she strokes Butter's head. Then she picks her up and carries her away.

Tears pour down my cheeks as I stare at the empty space.

Addie and Mercedes come and stand beside me. One on each side, trying to comfort me with their presence, but I'm inconsolable. Gloria has stolen my heart, and I'll never get it back.

DEGREES OF A BROKEN HEART

I don't feel well. I haven't all day. Mom brought me soup and ginger ale in bed, so I must really be sick. I keep the thermometer near me and take my temperature at regular intervals. It always measures the same 98.6, but a thermometer can't measure the degree of a broken heart.

I stare out the window at Butter's enclosure and wonder if she's okay. If I could only see her and know she's being well cared for, I'd feel a little better.

Mom knocks on my door. She comes in without me inviting her in. She's been in and out all day, checking on me, bringing me snacks and trying to coax me out. I'm mad at her, and she knows it. She never wanted me to have Butter in the first place, and she finally got her wish.

"You have some visitors." She steps back from the door.

Addie, Mercedes, and Theo walk in my room. All three are dressed in their ballet clothes. They sure do have a lot on their plates. Busy. Busy. Busy.

Mercedes sits on my bed. "Dress rehearsals are starting soon. I roped my little brother into dressing up like a goat. It's not the same as having Butter in the play, I know, but we still need you.

"You're our Peter," Theo says.

They don't know what they're asking. Without Butter, I'm not brave and I'm not different. I'm the same old Marvel who worries about everything and gets stage fright so badly I turn to stone. "I'm sorry. I can't do it. Not without Butter. I'll freeze up and ruin the play. Besides there's no reason for me to be up there anyway. Anyone can play him now. Without Butter, none of it matters."

Addie rubs my arm. "It matters to us."

I feel a lump rise in my throat, and I swallow it down. I push everything down. "You'll have to get someone to take over for me."

"But we want *you*," Mercedes says. "We need you."

I sit up. "I can't without Butter. Just give me my old townsperson part back. I'll do that to make Principal Huxx happy, but not the other part."

Mercedes says, "If you change your—"

I don't even let her finish. "I won't." My answer is final.

None of us seem to know what to say after that. Finally, Mercedes says, "We have to go. We have dance class."

When they get to the door, Addie turns. "Will we see you at school on Monday?"

"I don't think so." If I have my way, I'm never going back there.

I don't get my way.

———

Sunday evening, Dad comes into my room.

I'm at my computer. I've been googling *Can you die of heartbreak?*

He peers over my shoulder and looks at the screen, but doesn't comment on the content. "Ready for school tomorrow?"

Dad's words cause dread to coil in my stomach and make me feel really sick. "I could homeschool and do all my courses online. You know how good I am with the computer and research."

"Hiding from the world isn't the answer." Dad's voice has that parental confidence that screams *I know best*.

I swivel in my desk chair to face him. "Without Butter to come home to, I can't go back there."

"I know you don't want to. But sometimes that's life. We do things even when we don't want to, and in this case you don't have a choice. Principal Huxx said no more absences or you're going to fail."

"Maybe you could call her and explain the situation," I suggest, hoping Dad will take pity on me and arrange for me to stay home.

Dad shakes his head. "Sorry, honey."

I sigh. They're going to make me go.

"Once you get there, you might find you're glad you returned."

"I won't," I say, knowing without a doubt that it's true.

"Sweetheart, I know you're sad, but life has to move forward. So, tomorrow. School." Dad slaps his hands on his thighs and stands up. Decision rendered.

———

As promised, Mom wakes me up in time to get ready for school. No more ginger ale and soup in my room. My mourning period is over even though I'm still hurting.

"Are you walking today?" Mom asks cheerily, like nothing is wrong.

I glare at her. She knows I can't walk to school without Butter. "No."

"Okay, then!" Mom says, chirpy and happy like an annoying parakeet. "I'll grab my keys."

She drives me through the car line to drop me off.

Principal Huxx pulls open the car door. I step out, and she slams it shut. Mom waves as she drives away, but I don't return the gesture. I know I should, but I don't. I'll forgive her eventually. Just not today.

"Your father called to tell me about Butter," Principal Huxx says, peering at me with her authoritative glare, and I wonder if I'm somehow in trouble with her for bringing someone else's pet to school.

"Yeah," I say, filling the awkward silence that flares between us.

"I'm sorry to hear it. Butter seemed to help you become the person the rest of us know you to be." She's curt but caring, and the unexpected kind compliment from her makes my eyes well with tears.

"Thanks," I say.

She pats me on the shoulder and then snaps back into her normal self. "Get to class before the bell. You can't afford to be late."

I have language arts first again. I sit down at my table. Addie, Mercedes, and Theo pull their chairs close to mine. Other than their weirdly close proximity, they act normal, which is nice because it doesn't require too much from me and that's good because I'm too miserable to make conversation.

The day drags on and on. Everyone but me wants to talk about Butter. When lunchtime rolls around I go to the library instead of meeting Addie, Theo, and Mercedes on the playground. There's no point without Butter.

After school, I go to the auditorium for play practice.

Mercedes is both directing and playing Peter. Her

younger brother crawls around on the stage trying to bleat like a goat. Everyone is moving on but me.

I take my place with the townsfolk and try to blend in until practice ends. There are two weeks until the performance, and I can't wait for it to be over.

Near the end of practice, Dad comes in carrying the final pieces of the set. When Dad sees me, he smiles broadly and comes over. "Want me to wait for you until you're done? We can walk home together."

"That's okay. Mom's coming to pick me up."

"I know. She mentioned it, but we could call her to let her know you're walking. I have her number on speed dial." Dad nudges me playfully.

I know I'm disappointing him, but I shake my head. It's too sad to walk home with Dad without Butter. Nothing is the same without her.

When play practice is over, I go outside to wait for Mom to come get me and take me away from school, the play, and everything I became with Butter by my side.

After dinner, I sit in her enclosure and refuse to leave. It smells of hay, lavender, and wood; it smells of Butter.

I must have fallen asleep because I feel Dad's arms scoop me up to carry me inside. At first, I don't remember what's wrong. Then it all comes back. I shut my eyes as quickly as I can. I don't want to remember. I don't want to feel the emptiness in my heart.

I sit on my bed with my knees drawn close to my chest and stare out the window. It overlooks the garden. Through my curtains, I see Butter's enclosure, the home Dad built just for her.

My sadness is heavy like a thing, not a feeling, and I want it to go away. I want to forget it. Never think about it again, but if I do, I forget Butter.

Dad comes into my room and sits on the edge of my bed. He's quiet for a minute, waiting for me to turn toward him. Instead, I stare out the window. He finally says, "I've got some bad news, kiddo. I've been called back to my ship. I need to leave for San Diego first thing in the morning."

Dad's words tear my already-broken heart more. I don't understand why I have to say goodbye to him too. I lay my head on his shoulder. I've gotten used to leaning on it. "I don't want you to go."

"I know. I'll be back," Dad says.

"It could be months," I tell him. Months of missing him all the time, of no new memories, no day-to-day. He'll fade again like before and become an imaginary character in a faraway land. I don't want a hero for a father. I just want him home with me all the time.

"I don't want to go either, but I have to."

I finally look at him. "Last time, it was almost a year." We both know it's true. Almost a year is a long time. It's the difference between sixth grade and seventh. Kid and teenager. The difference between happy and sad.

"I know this is hard. Sometimes life just is."

"I wish you hadn't spent all that time with Butter and me if you weren't going to stay." I pull away and wrap my hands around my knees again, closing up.

"You don't mean that."

"I do. Everything's going back to the way it was before Butter." With Butter at my side life got bigger. I found friends, and Dad came home. Now it's shrinking back up again.

"It doesn't have to. Not if you don't let it." Dad takes my hand.

"I got used to you, and now you're leaving. Butter's gone too."

"I know it's heartbreaking, honey. We've got to take the good with the bad. Without the goodbyes, there are no joyful hellos."

Tears flow down my cheeks.

Dad sits with me and holds my hand. When the tears slow, he kisses the top of my head. "You have to feel it all. Without feeling the bad, you close yourself off to the good—the joy, the excitement, the wonder. You have to let it all flow through you. You can't bottle up the bad and think the good will somehow get in."

I sniff and bury my head into his chest. I hang on tight,

not wanting to let him go. "I'm going to miss you."

"I'm going to miss you too. You have no idea how much." Dad's voice turns gruff and scratchy. "But home is where your heart is, Marvel. And my heart is always here with you, your mom, and your brother. So, I'm always at home, even when I'm away."

Mom comes to my bedroom door. She sighs softly.

Dad glances over my head at Mom. His chin rests on the top of my head, and I can feel it move when he talks. "Your mom's going to videotape the play for me. My scenery is going to look *sick* on film."

Reef comes to the door and drapes his arm over Mom's shoulders. He's way taller than her now. Everything keeps changing. "*Sick*, dad? No one your age should say that."

Dad chuckles. "No, probably not. Hey, watch out for your sister while I'm away."

"Don't worry, Dad. We got her," Reef says.

Dad squeezes me tight and then lifts my chin to look me in the eye. "Only you can decide if you're going to perform the bigger role or not. If you decide not to, let it be for something else. Don't let it be because you were afraid to try."

His words swirl around me. It's good advice.

I wish I knew how to take it.

BRAVERY 101

With Dad and Butter gone, the house is really quiet. Mom misses Dad, and it's hard for me to watch. I wonder if Dad is her Butter, and she's not quite right without him. She keeps telling me we'll get back into the swing of things soon, and I guess we will. I don't suppose we have another option.

Reef's been hanging out with me more than usual. I think he's trying to take care of me like he promised Dad.

We sit at the kitchen table doing homework. We're both working on math. Only, his looks really complicated, like some sort of technical magic, and for some reason, it makes me think about life and feelings and ways of being. It makes me think that when it comes to who you are, unlike in math, there are no right answers.

"Is it hard for you with Dad gone?" I ask him.

Reef looks up. He's always the joker and nothing ever seems to get him down, so it never occurred to me to ask him before. "Sometimes. It's always hardest the first few days after he leaves. It's like trying to recalibrate an engine."

Reef wants to be an engineer. He's constantly thinking about how things work. Only, I'm not sure I get it. "What do you mean?"

He shrugs. "I get used to having him around, and it takes a few days before I remember he won't be here when I walk in the door or that I have to save something I want to tell him for when he calls."

"Yeah, I get that. I didn't really remember what it was like having him home all the time. It was nice having us all together."

"He'll be back."

"How do you know? His job is really dangerous."

Reef stares off into space for a second, thinking. He looks back at me. "I don't know. I suppose you can think about the worst-case scenario and focus on that or you can think of the best case. Either way you're trying to predict the future, which isn't possible."

What he says makes sense. I'm not sure how he does it, though. I don't know how he controls his thoughts. I can't stop thinking about what Dad told me. That he gets afraid but forges ahead anyway. "Dad said he gets scared all the time, but he doesn't let his fear make his decisions for him."

"That sounds like Dad. I don't know anyone who doesn't get scared."

I fiddle with my notebook. "It helps me to know that other people get worried about things. I think my fears have been in my mind so much that I thought it was just me and everyone else had it figured out."

Reef rubs the top of my head in a VERY annoying big-brother way. "No one I know has anything figured out."

I duck my head away from his aggressive petting. "One of the things I love so much about Butter is that even though she faints when things scare her, she doesn't let it stop her. She pops back up and keeps going."

Reef stares at me. "You're like that."

I'm completely taken aback by this observation. "What do you mean?"

"I see you getting knocked down a lot. Every time, you hop back up and keep going."

I didn't realize Reef had been paying attention to me. "But I get knocked down by stuff that other people find simple like going to school, giving speeches, or not worrying about every tiny thing, so it doesn't count."

"Are you sure about that?" he asks, looking at me with eyes so similar to Dad's it's like a lesson in genetics.

I guess I'm not. I fiddle with my pencil, tearing pieces of the eraser apart.

Reef watches me for a second and then says, "But I also think you're brave in the regular way too."

I stop pulling my eraser apart and peer up at him.

"You rescued Butter from those kids, brought her into Mom's garden, took her to school without Principal Huxx's permission . . . you also stole my scrimmage pinnie and cut it up to make a jacket for a goat. *That* definitely took guts." He punches my arm, and it's a smidge harder than it has to be to land his joke. "From my perspective, you're about as brave as they come."

I think about what he says, trying to see myself through his eyes. I did do all those things, but because I *had* to do them. I didn't have any other choice. "The pinnie looked better on her than it ever did on you," I tell him, and punch him back, but lightly, kind of like a hug.

"True," he says, and goes back to doing homework and I do the same, but I can't stop thinking about his words. For the rest of the evening, they blow around my head like seeds in the wind until they eventually settle and start to sprout.

GROUP

Group therapy meets in the school basement, a location that makes me nervous. I worry that if there is an earthquake, the building will collapse and trap me. Possibly kill me. I know it might sound silly to someone else, but the danger feels very real to me. In fact, it feels so likely to happen that I replay disaster-response scenarios over and over in my mind.

The last few days, Mr. J and I have been talking about it A LOT. He's helping me realize that my concern isn't rational. Yesterday, he encouraged me to write a list of facts to challenge my fear.

I stand at the door to the basement and pull the list out of my pocket. I reread it.

My Fear: An Earthquake Will Cause the Building to Collapse and KILL ME.

1. The construction of our school is fairly new and has up-to-date safety standards. (This does make me feel better.)

2. I'll only be in the basement for one hour a week. The likelihood that a major earthquake will happen in that one hour is not very probable. (I'm not a math genius, but this makes sense.)

3. If an earthquake is going to occur, it will happen no matter where I am. Going into the basement will not make an earthquake happen. (That's logically sound.)

4. There are several exit doors in the basement. (I did not know this previously. Mr. J got out a map and pointed them out to me.)

It's a good list. It puts my mind at ease, so I am going to do it.

I slip the emergency whistle I swiped from our earthquake go bag over my head and tuck it under my shirt. I didn't tell Mr. J I planned to wear it *just in case*. He doesn't need to know everything. Baby steps.

To my surprise, the basement looks a lot better than I imagined. It's carpeted, well lit, and very clean. It also has a few windows on one side. I mean, it's not just pleasant. It's really nice.

All of a sudden, I feel silly. I avoided group because I was afraid of the basement, and it's not even scary.

This group isn't the same as our school friendship group. That group isn't real therapy; this group is, and that's part of the problem with it. I don't like the idea of sharing my private thoughts with other kids my age. That's terrifying, but Mr. J said I didn't have to say anything at all. I could just listen.

There are five of us: me, a girl named Bree (she's in a different homeroom), a boy named Chris (I think he might be from a different school because I don't know him), another girl named Makayla (also from another school, I think), and Jamie (this completely surprises me).

The only seat open is next to Jamie, so I reluctantly sit there and whisper to him, "I didn't know you came to this group." I'm pretty sure we can talk, but everyone else is really quiet. I don't want to be the only one chatting.

He shrugs. "Since the beginning of the school year."

I want to ask him what he's in for, but that seems kind of rude.

Jamie uncharacteristically offers the information. "My parents got divorced at the beginning of the year. They still fight a lot. It's not easy."

I gape at him, stunned by his honest confession.

"Stop staring at me like I have two heads. You'll find out soon enough anyway because this is group and everyone shares everything, but you're not allowed to judge or tell anybody else, so I don't care if you know."

"I would never say anything even if there wasn't a rule against it," I promise.

Jamie squints at me and then nods appreciatively.

Mr. J calls the group to order, and it's nothing like I thought. It's just us kids chatting, and I'm surprised at how much it helps. Makayla also has anxiety, and parts of her brain work a lot like mine. Listening to her talk makes me feel less alone, and that makes my fears seem smaller somehow. I think I'm going to like coming here.

After group, Jamie and I walk outside. I'd be lying if I said I wasn't relieved to be aboveground again, but it's a small thought. Not a big, huge one that feels like it's going to grab hold of my brain like a ravenous zombie and not let go.

"You want to walk home together?" Jamie asks, completely shocking me. "I live close to you." My face must show my astonishment because he says, "Ugh. You're so annoying, *Frosty*. We're not going to be best friends or anything like that. It's pure convenience, and Mr. J told me to try to be more cordial three times a week. This counts as one."

It's not the most complimentary invitation, and I

haven't walked home alone since Butter went away. "My mom is supposed to pick me up."

"You can use my cell phone to call her." He takes out his phone and hands it to me.

Everyone has a phone but me. Mom and I really need to have a conversation about this.

I take his phone and stare at it for a moment. Then I punch in the number.

Today is full of big steps.

ANYTHING FOR LOVE

As soon as I walk in the door, I hear our phone ringing. I swear we're the only people on the planet to still have a landline. No one else is home. Reef is at an elite, overnight soccer tournament and Mom is at her landscaping job.

I lunge for the phone. "Hello?"

There's a delay, and then the other line crackles. Robocall.

I'm about to hang up when someone says, "Is this Marvel?"

The voice sounds familiar. I know I should recognize the caller, but I can't quite place her. "May I ask who's calling, please?"

"This is Gloria Fizzle, Butter's owner. I'm trying to reach Marvel."

Hearing Butter's name makes me ache with longing. "This is Marvel."

"Thank goodness I've reached you," Gloria says in a rush. "It's Butter. She's not doing well. She's stopped eating and drinking. I've tried everything I can think of. Nothing has helped."

My heart lurches. "But . . . why?"

"I've been asking myself that very same question. This morning I told the vet about you. She thinks Butter is grieving. Goats are social creatures and bond closely with the people they love. She misses you."

"I miss her too."

"Could you come to my barn and try to coax her into eating?" Gloria sounds desperate.

"My mom would have to drive me, but she's not home yet. Can I call you right back?"

"Do you have a pen?" Gloria asks. I dig around the kitchen for one and something to write on. Gloria gives me all the details and tells me to call her back once I know if I can get there. "Please don't take too long. I'm not sure how much time Butter has."

Her words shock me. "She's that sick?"

"I'm afraid so," Gloria says, her distress clear.

I grip the phone, trying to hang on to something solid. The idea of a world without Butter in it doesn't make any sense to me. I hang up with Gloria and dial Mom, but it takes me a few tries to get the number correct because neither my mind nor hands are working properly and I keep messing up. When I finally get her number dialed, she picks up on the first ring.

"Mom?" My voice sounds like one a much younger me would use.

"Honey, what's wrong?"

"It's Butter—" I break off, unable to get the words out. They're too terrible, and I'm crying too hard to speak.

"Sweetheart, take a deep breath and try again." Mom's voice sounds calm, but I hear worry underneath her composure.

I do as she says, and I'm finally able to fill her in on everything and give her Gloria's address.

"I'm on my way but . . ." She pauses for a moment like she doesn't want to finish her sentence. Then she continues, "It's Friday afternoon. Bay Area traffic is notorious. It'll take a couple of hours to get home this time of day. If not more."

I go silent. I didn't turn on the lights when I walked in the door, and I regret it now. As the sun sinks outside, the dimming natural light makes our usually cozy kitchen feel bleak and lonely. I imagine Butter alone in a darkening enclosure, thin and frail, bleating for me, and me not answering her calls. The picture makes me frantic to get to her as quickly as possible, but I don't have a way there.

On the other end of the line, I hear Mom's car door slam. "I'm coming home now. I'll get there as fast as I can. You know . . ." Mom trails off, thoughtful, and I can tell she has an idea she wants to share.

"Yeah?" I ask. Normally, I'd never encourage her to continue because it usually means she's going to suggest something I'm not going to like, but this concerns Butter.

"The address Gloria gave is in the headlands. There's a bus that goes out there. Reef rode it to his camp counselor job last summer. If you took it, you wouldn't have to wait for me, and it'd be fast. The bus gets to use the carpool lane, but I know how you feel about taking it, especially by yourself."

I hate the bus. The schedule is a confusing puzzle of numbers and tables and all the buses look identical. The only thing that differentiates one from another is the tiny numbers in the front window, which are informative as long as the numbers are updated, but what if someone forgets? I could accidently get on a bus headed in the wrong direction. Even if I do get on the correct one, I have to ring the bell at the right time so the driver knows when to stop. If not, I might end up miles from where I meant to go, maybe even as far away as another state. I also need a bus card or the exact fare, which has to be put in the automated collection box, and those machines are finicky. Anything too crinkled gets spit right back out.

I bite my bottom lip. Taking the bus alone feels as daunting as swimming across San Francisco Bay.

"Marvel? Are you there?"

"Yes," I say as my mind grapples with my choices, which boil down to waiting for Mom or taking the bus. Being a coward or being brave.

"I'll get home as soon as I can," Mom says. I hear her start the car, but she won't make it here fast enough. I imagine Butter's sweet face, gaunt and haggard from not eating. She needs me immediately, not two or three hours from now.

I can't let imaginary fears prevent me from helping Butter. I love her too much. "Mom, I don't think I should wait. Butter needs me to go now . . ." I pause, wondering if I can actually do it.

"It's your choice, honey."

Trying to shift through my warring emotions, I say, "Dad gets scared sometimes."

"I know, everyone does."

"But he doesn't let his fear make his decisions for him. He says a life lived in fear isn't really living."

"Your dad is very wise."

Mom's right. Dad is wise, and I know what I have to do. "I'm going to take the bus. Can you meet me at Gloria's?"

"You know I will," Mom says, and I think I understand something else about being brave. Courage comes from many sources, the most powerful of which is love.

"Thanks, Mom."

"Anytime. Remember, you get off at Fort Cronkhite. Text me when you get there."

I roll my eyes. Has Mom forgotten I don't have a cell phone? "On what?"

"There's a present for you in my closet. We were going to give it to you at the end of the year, but I think you better take it. It's a cell phone. It should be charged. Reef set it up and insisted we plug it in. You know how obsessed he is with technology."

I don't even have time to be excited about finally getting a cell phone. I'm too worried about Butter and the bus.

I hang up with Mom and call Gloria to tell her I'm on my way. She promises to meet me at the bus stop near her barn.

I pull up the schedule online and print it out. I figure out what bus to take, dig around for exact change, grab my new cell phone from Mom's closet, and leave for the bus stop.

The stop is across the street from the pet store and even though it's close to my house, I run the whole way. The next bus out to the headlands is due soon and if I miss it, I have to wait thirty minutes for the next one.

I round the corner, see the stop up ahead and the back of a bus as it pulls away. I run faster, waving my arms over my head to make the driver stop, but it's useless. It speeds away, leaving me behind.

Frustration makes me so angry, I kick a bench.

I immediately regret it. Now my toes throb on top of everything else. I plop down on the bench and check the schedule against the time. My mind unravels a string of what-ifs. *What if that was the last one? What if they've suspended all service to the headlands? What if the bus I need broke down or has a flat tire? What if I never make it to Butter?*

I know I'm catastrophizing (always assuming the worst), and while I can't quite stop it, I think Mr. J would be proud of me for identifying one of my patterns and acknowledging it.

Despite my flash of insight, my stomach churns as I watch the road, willing a bus to come.

I'm so focused on looking out for the next one that I flinch when someone taps me on the shoulder and shouts, "MARVEL?"

I spin around and find Goth Girl smiling at me. She's wearing a pair of purple combat boots and I think she's added a face piercing.

"Hey," I say, pleased to see her friendly face.

She sits down next to me. "Where are you going? Why isn't Butter with you?"

At the mention of Butter, my eyes sting with tears. I tell her all about Gloria, Butter, and needing to take the bus because my mom is stuck in traffic.

Goth Girl listens to it all. To her credit, she's kind enough not to mention she warned me that Butter might have a caring owner who wanted her back.

"Is it your first time taking the bus alone?" she asks, louder than necessary, but I don't care. It's comforting to talk to her. She knows what it's like to love an animal with your whole heart.

I nod and twist the schedule, mangling it.

She glances at my frantic hands. "I take the bus all the time. Want me to take a look? It can be confusing."

I hand her the schedule and she goes over it with me. She even helps me download an app with all the routes and traffic updates on my new cell phone.

"It should be here in . . . well, now." Goth Girl points to a bus coming toward us.

It stops and I check its number against the schedule to make sure it's the right bus. I confirm that it's the correct one and then verify it again for good measure.

The driver opens the doors.

"Good luck, Marvel. Give Butter a hug for me," Goth Girl says.

"I will," I say, and step on the bus.

REUNITED

I carefully feed a dollar into the automated collection box near the driver and then thread a second one through the machine. While I wait to make sure the contraption swallows it, I take the opportunity to confirm the route one more time. "You stop at Fort Cronkhite in the headlands, right?"

The driver gives me a nod, but I want verbal confirmation.

"So, that's a yes?" I smile at him to let him know I'm not trying to be difficult.

"Yup," he says, and pulls the lever to close the doors. They shut behind me with a swish and I survey the long rows of seats, trying to strategize the best place to sit. There aren't many other people on the bus, giving me a lot of options.

I finally decide on the very first row, so I can look out the front window to watch for my stop, but not the seat right behind the driver. His seat will block my view. I pick the one on the other side.

I plop into it and the bus starts to move. I wonder if I'm allowed to ask the driver questions since I'm sitting close to him. Probably not.

The bus pulls onto the highway. I lean back, sighing, relieved to finally be on my way to Butter.

We speed along in the carpool lane, flying past bumper-to-bumper traffic. Mom was right. This will be fast.

We drive through the Robin Williams Tunnel. I suck in a deep breath and hold it until we're out for good luck. All the kids I know do it.

On the other side of the tunnel, we hit the fog. A heavy, white blanket envelops us and makes San Francisco look like it's floating in the clouds. Up ahead, I see the Golden Gate Bridge and the exit that will take us into the headlands instead of the city.

My heart beats faster with impatience. The closer we get, the more anxious I am to see Butter. I'm also nervous about pressing the button. I don't want to make a mistake and not do it in enough time to alert the driver. If I push it too late, he'll cruise right past my stop.

The driver takes the exit for the headlands. Views of San Francisco dissolve as rolling hills replace cityscape.

It's almost time for me to hit the button. I examine it warily. I hope it works properly and wonder if I should test it.

Tentatively, I stretch out my hand and lightly press it as an experiment.

A bell chimes and the bus driver glances at me in the rearview mirror. He slows the bus and pulls over at a deserted stop just off the highway exit.

It's not mine and I wonder what I should do. I twist around and look at the other passengers. Maybe one of them needs to get off. No one moves.

He pulls open the door and looks at me, raising his eyebrows. "Did you want to exit?"

I lean forward in my seat and ask a question I already know the answer to in an effort to camouflage my anxiety-driven action. "Is this Fort Cronkhite?"

"Nope. Next stop."

I smile at him apologetically. "Sorry, that one, then."

He pulls the doors closed and merges back onto the road.

Grimacing, I immediately reach up and press the button again, making another bell sound.

The driver glances at me in his rearview mirror. I smile self-consciously and wave.

At the next stop, he pulls over and opens the door. This location is deep in the headlands, but there's a crop of white buildings with red roofs and an older lady waiting by the side of the road. Gloria Fizzle.

Gloria bustles over and hands me a thermos of hot chocolate and wraps a thick barn coat around my shoulders. "It gets cold out here after dark."

I snuggle into the coat and clutch the thermos. "Thank you."

"I'm so grateful you made the trip," Gloria says, and leads me toward her barn.

"I appreciate you calling me. I would do anything for Butter."

"I know." She pats my arm with her hand. "The day I came to claim Butter, I felt terrible separating the two of you. I shouldn't have done it. That little goat is lovesick."

"I understand why you did," I say. "If I had lost her, I'd want her back too."

When we get to the barn, the vet, Dr. Harman, waits for us outside Butter's stable.

Dr. Harman appears to be about Mom's age and skips formalities, launching right into an explanation about Butter's condition. "Goats are social animals. They form deep connections with members of their herd and can die of loneliness. However, I've never seen anything quite like this. Goats don't typically form this type of connection with a human. They usually prefer to live with other goats."

Dr. Harman pulls back the stable door. Inside, Butter lies on her side. She doesn't look right. She looks smaller than I remember, and she pants. An IV to keep her hydrated is taped to one of her legs, but instead of being reassuring, it makes her seem even more tiny and frail.

I bite back tears. I can't reconcile the delicate creature before me with my memories of bouncy, energetic Butter. I want to drop to my knees and cradle her in my arms, but I fight the urge because the vet is still filling me in on her condition.

"The IV is not a permanent solution. Butter needs to eat on her own. I should have removed it already, but Gloria asked me to keep it in until you got here. This is one lucky little goat. A lot of people love her," Dr. Harman says.

I sit down next to Butter, but I'm not sure she knows it's me at first. I glance up at Dr. Harman, wondering what I should do.

"Try talking to her," Dr. Harman says. "She's not quite herself."

"Butter. It's Marvel. I'm here. I'm—" I choke on my tears and lay my face on top of hers.

She finally seems to realize it's me. She bleats weakly and wags her tail.

I kiss her pink nose and stroke her ears. "Silly girl. Why aren't you eating?"

Dr. Harman removes the IV. "It's up to Butter now."

Butter snuggles her head into my lap and I stroke her side, doing my best to soothe her.

I don't know how long Gloria and Dr. Harman stand outside the stall watching over us. I only have eyes for Butter.

I caress her head and tell her some of the things I'm slowly starting to learn. "You know, life doesn't have to be scary."

Butter bleats softly.

"It's true. Before I met you, everything frightened me—global warming, earthquakes, school, tests, other kids. You remember, I told you all about it. Then you came into my life, and everything got easier."

Butter sighs and tilts her head toward me, exposing the underside of her chin. I gently scratch it.

"When you left, I went back to being afraid. But Dad told me I could be scared and brave at the same time. I didn't believe him at first, but I think I do now. I also started working with Mr. J and he's been teaching me skills for dealing with my anxiety. I think it's helping or will help if I keep practicing."

She leans her head against my chest, and my whole being explodes with love for her.

I continue to pet Butter and tell her everything I've learned from Dad, Mom, Reef, Mr. J, the kids at school, and especially her.

I hand-feed her some grain. She takes little bites but doesn't really eat. She seems too weak to even try. "Butter, you need to eat. You have to get better. I love you."

Butter tips her face toward mine and nibbles on a little bit of my hair, and I know she feels exactly the same about me.

When it's so dark Gloria has to turn on barn lights, Mom shows up.

She wraps me in a huge hug. She smells like potting soil and mulch. She's always there when I need her, and I realize how much I love her.

Mom stopped at the deli on the way out and bought me dinner—a grilled cheese sandwich and a cup of tomato soup. My favorite meal. She sits with us while I eat. We don't say too much to each other, but having Mom there and feeling the warmth of her next to me make me feel better. I hope Butter feels the same way about me.

When I finish my dinner, Mom says, "Gloria offered to put us up for the evening. I don't suppose I'm going to be able to talk you into coming inside to sleep?"

I look down at Butter. Her ragged breathing makes her side move up and down unnaturally labored. "I can't leave her."

"I didn't think so. Gloria gave me some blankets for you." Mom wraps a couple of stable blankets around my arms. "I'm going to let you have some time alone with

Butter. I'll check on you both periodically. Dr. Harman will be back to examine Butter in the morning." Mom kisses the top of my head and leaves.

After Mom goes, I offer Butter sips of water from my hand and keep trying until she laps up a little bit. Encouraged by my success with the water, I stay up late feeding Butter grain, one piece at a time.

Then I wrap the blanket around me and snuggle up to her. She lifts her head and looks at me, but she doesn't have any of her old spark left. We lie there for a long time. I listen to the sounds of the barn—other goats bleating and an owl hooting. I also concentrate on the sound of Butter's breathing. It's a slow in-and-out that makes me drowsy. I do my best to stay awake, but at some point, I slip into sleep like going down a slide.

———

It takes a minute to remember where I am. The sun is shining down on me, and hay is stuck to my face. Then it all comes slamming back.

As soon as I think about Butter, I sit bolt upright. She's not next to me. My heart starts pounding as fear surges through my body, and then I see her.

Butter's nibbling on hay and drinking water on her own.

I scramble up and throw my arms around her. "Butter, you're okay!"

Mom comes into the enclosure. "Good morning,

sleepyhead. We thought you might never wake up. Apparently, stable life agrees with you."

"Mom! Butter's eating!" I grin so wide it makes my cheeks hurt.

"I know! She started to perk up around six this morning. Dr. Harman checked her out and gave her a good prognosis."

"I slept through it all?" I'm horrified at myself. I'm going to make a terrible parent.

"You stayed awake for the tough part, and you pulled her through. I'm really proud of you. You saved Butter's life."

"It's only fair. She saved mine," I say.

Mom hugs me.

I look at Butter. "You know, I might not ever get over my anxiety completely."

"You might not," Mom agrees.

"It might always be a part of me, but I think now I understand it doesn't have to be the biggest part." As soon as I say it, I know it's true.

32

THE SHOW MUST GO ON

After Butter finishes her breakfast and I eat something, Gloria takes Mom and me on a tour of her property.

Her barn and the surrounding land look more like an idyllic movie set than a real-life place. The barn sits on top of a hill overlooking San Francisco Bay, with views expanding outward onto sky, sea, and city. Gloria points out trails leading down to the beach and tells me about the saltwater pools that form at high tide.

As we walk, fog clings to the ground, creating a dreamy mist around my feet, and all around me, wide, rolling fields of fresh grass extend for miles. There are also goats.

Tons and tons of goats.

Once Butter started eating and drinking on her own again, she perked up and now bounces beside me as we follow Gloria around her property. Butter sniffs at a wild-flower, disturbing a bee, and jumps back. Mom, Gloria, and I laugh at her.

My heart blooms with happiness watching Butter behave like her normal, bouncy self, and I know for certain that even if I could spend a thousand years observing her, I would never grow tired of it.

I slip my hand in Mom's and lean my head on her arm as we walk. I'm mostly happy, but a little sad too because soon I'll have to leave Butter again. Mom squeezes my hand like she understands the mixture of happiness and heartbreak tugging at me, and I suppose she does. Mom and Dad have had a lot of reunions and a lot of goodbyes. All of us have.

I let go of her hand and run through the field with Butter, letting myself enjoy our time together while it lasts.

About halfway through our tour, we lose Mom. She gets enthralled by the variety of plants that grow around the barn and wanders away for a self-guided tour of the flora and fauna.

"Your mom really likes plants," Gloria says with the same dismay I feel at Mom's obsession.

I tuck my hands into my back pockets and watch her go. "She does. As much as I like goats."

Gloria smiles at me like she understands and approves

of my fascination with the bouncy creatures. "Would you like to help me feed them?"

"I'd love to." I'm thrilled to accept her offer and spend the next hour helping Gloria around the barn. The whole time I work, Butter prances alongside me and I try to memorize all her details—the markings on her fur, the exact shape and color of her eyes, and the way she bounces—so I can remember her perfectly later.

While we work, Gloria asks me questions about Butter's time at my house. I tell her about finding Butter, taking her to school, and the play. In return, Gloria tells me all about the goats and her life. By the time we're done with the chores, I know Butter is in good hands with her. She's really nice and loves her goats. If Butter can't be with me, I'm glad she's with Gloria.

Mom comes back from her wanderings and I ask her the time before I realize I can look at my very own cell phone. I pull it out of my back pocket and my eyes well up because my time at this perfect place and with Butter is up. The play starts in a couple of hours, and if I'm not there, I'm going to fail sixth grade. "Mom, it's Saturday."

"I know, and what a great place to spend it." Mom stares dreamily out at the view, completely misunderstanding my meaning. Some people get lost in the clouds, but not Mom. For her, it's plants. She totally loses herself in them.

"Mom, *the play*. I'm supposed to be at school in . . ." I look at the time on my phone again. "Two hours."

Mom snaps out of it. "Gracious. I totally forgot."

"If I don't get there, I'm done for. Meaning, I fail sixth grade. Remember?"

"I know. I know," Mom says, and frantically starts gathering our things.

I extend my hand to Gloria, trying to handle this goodbye more maturely than the last. "Thanks for calling me and for having such a great home for Butter. I feel better knowing she gets to live at this wonderful place."

Gloria takes my hand in hers, but instead of a formal handshake, she cradles it between both of her hands in a very grandmotherly way, making me wish I was related to her so I could visit again. "Thanks for coming when I called you. Butter's lucky to have you."

"I'd do anything for her." At the mention of Butter and how much I love her, my eyes pool with tears. I hate having to say goodbye to Butter all over again. Knowing she's going to be well taken care of makes it a little easier but not much. My heart still aches with the finality of it, and I want to put off my goodbye to her until the very last second.

I turn and walk toward our car as Butter bounces along beside me.

I'm almost there when Gloria says, "Marvel, wait."

I turn back around. "Yes?"

"Would you like to help me out around here on weekends? I could meet you at the bus stop and walk you back here. There's a lot to do around this place, and I could use the help."

I look over at Mom. She nods. Even though it means I'll have to ride the bus, I don't hesitate. A bus ride is nothing if I get to see Butter every weekend. It's not the same as having her by my side every day, but I'll take it. "I'd love that!"

"I only have one condition."

"Okay," I say warily. I'm not big on conditions. They usually end up being something I hate, and my mouth turns down, expecting an unpleasant stipulation.

"You have to bring Butter with you when you come."

"Bring Butter with me? I don't understand. Won't she be here?"

Gloria smiles. "No, she's going with you. That little goat has made it very clear what and who she needs."

I forget all about maturity and fling my arms around Gloria. "Thank you."

Mom gets misty-eyed and hugs Gloria too.

Gloria smiles. "Don't you have somewhere to be?"

"Yes!" I say. "See you next weekend!"

"See you next weekend," Gloria says.

Mom, Butter, and I scramble into the car. Mom pulls away from the barn, and I spin around in my seat so I can wave goodbye to Gloria. I watch her figure get smaller and smaller until we turn the corner and I lose sight of her. Then I settle Butter on my lap and roll down the car window so she can stick her head out.

As we drive along the isolated roads back to civilization, Mom tries to bore me to death by pointing to plants and reciting their Latin names, but I barely listen to her. Now that Butter's out of danger and coming home with me, my mind latches onto getting to the play and the time ticking by because the drive home seems to be taking longer than it should.

Mom stops cataloging plant life and leans forward over the steering wheel in concentration.

I watch her growing more and more anxious until I can't contain it any longer. "Are we lost?"

"Um . . . I think I know where I am, but maybe you could pop our home address into the GPS just to make sure we're on track?" Mom's tone is calm and confident like everything is completely fine. We're *definitely* lost.

I punch our address into the GPS and check the clock again. We have an hour and fifteen minutes to get there. We still have plenty of time.

We listen for the GPS to start guiding us, but it never does. We're too deep in the headlands for a cell signal.

Mom taps her finger on the car monitor in an old-lady attempt to make it work. "How can we be so close to the city yet out of range of cell towers? It makes no sense."

I stroke Butter to ease my skyrocketing anxiety. The headlands have not only deadened all the cell signals, they've also gobbled up our extra time.

"Mom, I can't miss the play." The tension in my voice doesn't even begin to express the panic consuming my thoughts.

"I know," she says, and then clams up to concentrate on the road.

She finally navigates her way back to civilization, but by the time we reach school, I'm an hour late for call time. Mercedes wanted the entire cast to arrive early for prep and will be livid I missed it, but I can deal with her. It's Principal Huxx I'm truly worried about. If she doesn't see me performing onstage, I'm going to fail and I don't have much time left before the curtain goes up.

Mom pulls up in front of the school to drop me off. "Should I take Butter home?"

I pause for a second, thinking. If I do the smaller part, I'll only have to blend in with the townspeople and stand there for a few seconds. The other choice is to take a risk and play Peter.

"Do you feel well enough to perform?" I ask Butter.

She bleats, and I take that for a yes.

"Does that mean what I think it means?" Mom asks.

"It does," I say, and hop out of the car to find Mercedes.

It's pandemonium backstage. The tech crew drags scenery around, kids struggle into costumes, and parents snap pictures. I spot Theo and go over to him.

"Where have you . . . ?" He stops mid-sentence when he realizes I'm holding Butter. He gives her a lavish, heartfelt greeting. "You clearly have a ton to fill me in on, but the play is starting in ten minutes, so you'll have to tell me later."

"Do you know where Mercedes is?"

He points to the stage. Mercedes stands in the middle of it shouting directions at people.

I go to her. "Mercedes?"

She spins around. "What?" she asks harshly, and then notices me holding Butter.

"Could you handle a couple of last-minute cast changes?" I ask timidly.

Mercedes throws her arms around me. "Could I ever. Give Butter to me and go get in your costume. Quickly. I think we still have her Cheerios around here some-where." She takes Butter away from me and pushes me in the direction of the dressing room.

After I'm changed, I see Jamie in a corner by himself. He's mumbling his lines over and over again. If I didn't know better, I'd think he was freaking out.

Mercedes brings Butter back and hands me a baggie of Cheerios. "You two ready?"

"We're ready," I say.

Mercedes calls everyone to their places and goes out to introduce the show. Then it starts.

The show opens with Addie, as Heidi, being dragged uphill by Aunt Dete, played by Theo. They're wonderful. Theo gets a lot of laughs, which I know he loves.

Before I'm truly ready, it's time for my entrance. The beginning is one of the worst parts. It's where Peter has the most lines. Butter comes out with me, and the audience shows silent appreciation for her by making hearts with their hands, the way Mercedes instructed in her pre-show speech.

The warmth of it drives away all my nerves, and I deliver my lines. Not perfectly but good enough.

Jamie's entrance is next. Only he doesn't come out on cue. He seems to be stuck backstage.

I say his cue line again, "Oh, Grandfather." But he doesn't come out.

I see Mercedes start to panic in the front row.

I look back to the stage wings and notice Jamie still hesitating.

Addie ad-libs a few lines. "Grandfather must be at the well. Go find him, Peter. GO!" she says dramatically, and shoves me offstage.

I stumble into the stage wings carrying Butter. "Jamie, you're supposed to be out there. What are you doing?" I hiss.

"I forgot my lines, dummy. I can't go out there and make a fool out of myself."

Good grief. Must he insult me when I'm trying to help? "You don't have a choice. You've got to get out there! Addie's good, but she can't ad-lib the entire scene."

"Just get back onstage, *Frosty*, and do a goat trick or something. I'll be out there in a minute. As soon as I remember my lines." He turns his back to me to concentrate, but it doesn't seem to be working.

From the stage, I hear Addie and Theo making up crazy dialogue. Mercedes must be losing it.

For some reason, I know if I leave without Jamie, he won't join us. He'll stay right where he is, and I'll end up having to ad-lib lines, which I am *totally* not up for. "Jamie, you know your lines. You've been saying them for weeks. You're just freaking out."

"I do not freak out! I'm not you, *Frosty*. Just give me one second."

"You don't have one second." I just heard Addie talking about flying to the moon and Theo has launched into a soliloquy on Aunt Dete's motivation for her bad behavior. He's started at the day of her birth. "The play is crashing and burning out there!"

"Just go. I'm right behind you."

He's totally not. "I think you're having some stage fright. Mercedes says it can happen to anyone, but the

300

panic you feel isn't real and I know exactly what to do. Hold your arms out."

He does, and I put Butter in his arms. He looks at her like she's a sea monster, not an adorable miniature goat. "How's *this* supposed to help?" he asks, irritated.

"Trust me. I'm an expert. Don't think about what's going to happen. Just think about Butter."

"If I make a fool of myself out there . . ."

"You can call yourself Frosty," I say sharply. "Now come on!" I drag him out onto the stage and say, "I found Grandfather!"

Jamie looks like a deer in headlights. But I watch him pull Butter close, snuggle into her, and then squeak out his lines.

Once he gets the first few words out of his mouth, he's apparently cured because he thrusts Butter back at me and starts to ham it up, stealing everyone else's spotlight. TOTAL DIVA. At least the play is officially under way.

The next forty-five minutes are a mixture of misery and excitement. When I'm onstage pretending to be Peter, I'm not thinking about much else, so it's fine. But in between scenes, I have to keep my anxiety in check by breathing deeply and focusing on Butter.

When the curtain finally comes down, I collapse into a chair backstage, thrilled it's finally over.

Jamie sees me. He comes over and begrudgingly says,

"Thanks for the save out there, *Frosty.*"

"You're welcome," I say with an irritability I don't truly feel, and I'm utterly surprised to find I'm no longer bothered by his nickname for me.

Addie, Theo, and Mercedes find me. They wrap me and Butter up in a very squishy, unstable group hug. We almost fall over and stumble into someone—Principal Huxx.

All four of us straighten up and get serious fast.

She looks down at us. "Mercedes, congratulations on a successful production. Addie, Theo, you both gave believable portrayals. Marvel, I must say, I was surprised to see your goat tonight." She pauses, and I wonder if I broke some kind of rule. "But I was glad to see her back. She added a little something special that really made this play a standout."

She turns and starts to walk away, while Addie, Mercedes, Theo, and I look at one another in stunned silence. Then she turns back. "I hope this means Butter will be joining you at school Monday morning."

My eyes get super big, and I nod. "She will."

After Principal Huxx leaves, Addie, Theo, Mercedes, and I link arms and walk offstage. Butter bounds ahead of us, leading the way.

ENCORE

I wait in the wings of the auditorium stage. Addie, Mercedes, Theo, and I hold hands. We're wearing matching ballet costumes for our recital. After the play ended, I signed up for dance class and discovered that the bigger my life gets—the more open I am to trying new things— the happier I am.

Addie leans close to me and sniffs. "You smell like hay."

I smile. "I was at Gloria's barn. I took the bus here."

Theo plucks a piece of straw from my hair and raises his eyebrows. "You know you're supposed to feed it *to* the goats, not wear it, right?"

Laughing, I nudge him in the side with my elbow. "*Really?* Good to know. Thanks for setting me straight."

Mercedes shushes us. "You're not supposed to talk

in the stage wings. Did I teach you three nothing?"

Addie, Theo, and I giggle, but stop chatting.

I peek into the audience. Mom and Reef sit in the front row, which probably annoys the person behind Reef. He's taller than ever.

A few rows behind them, Goth Girl sprawls out in an aisle seat with her legs stretched into the walkway. She's wearing pink combat boots and a fluffy tutu over black leggings. I grin at her, thrilled she accepted my invitation to the performance.

At first I don't see Dad, but then I spot him. He's standing at the back of the auditorium. He has shore duty now, so he goes to work during the day and comes home at night. It's great to have him home. I know he might have to leave again, and it will be sad, but I can handle it. I've been working hard with Mr. J.

Standing next to Dad is a four-legged audience member—Butter. Dad holds on to her leash, and she wears her red support vest.

I wave.

Dad waves back and gives me the thumbs-up signal.

The house lights flash.

"Ready, Marvel?" Addie asks.

I smile at her. I am nervous, but I work through it and, when the stage lights pop on, I walk into them.

ACKNOWLEDGMENTS

I'm deeply indebted to the magnificent Mallory Kass for believing a novel about a goat was a good idea. Her smart, savvy editorial helped me turn a proposal into an outline, the outline into a messy first draft, and then, finally, a book. With each pass, she made everything better. I am in awe of her brilliant brain and grateful for her huge heart.

I'm incredibly lucky to call the amazing Laura Rennert my agent and cherished friend. She is a loving, supportive, fierce advocate for all writers and a devoted individual who champions with her whole heart. I adore her beyond measure. I'm thankful for all the women of the Andrea Brown Literary Agency, but especially Andrea Brown, Caryn Wiseman, Jennifer March Soloway, Paige Terlip, and Alison Nolen, the Grammar Goddess. They are my literary family.

Special appreciation to Jennifer March Soloway, the Queen of Titles, for bestowing this book with the cutest name ever. More importantly, thank you for the treasure of friendship.

I don't know if I would be a writer without my sister Beth. She makes my stories better, and my life fuller. When I write, it's for her. I work hard to make her cry, but I love it most when I make her laugh.

Writing might be a solitary endeavor, but creating a book is a collaborative enterprise, and I'm very grateful for all the members of the Scholastic team. They work tirelessly on behalf of authors and readers, and fill the world with books. Special thanks to Assistant Editor Maya Marlette, Production Editor Mary Kate Garmire, Art Director Keirsten Geise, and Regional Key Account Manager Theresa Frei.

Marvel's anxiety journey is her singular experience, but I hope it also feels universal, and I appreciate Dr. Petey Kass for sharing his expertise, and Leslie Nobile and Lucia Nobile for providing their perspective.

There are so many people in my day-to-day life who encouraged me (probably more than they know) by asking about my first book and being excited about the next one, especially the kids: Sophia, Mirielle, Rebecca, Maria, Alexis, Alix, Soleil, Elin, Ylva, Harlow, Aven, Van, Braden, Drew, Caitlin, Mackie, Keirnan, Owen, and Kyra.

A deep, heartfelt thanks to the Kids Need Mentors students, and teachers Jennifer Kulp, Nicole Crome, and

Ronnae Forsyth, as well as all the teachers, librarians, and readers. Writers may create books, but you make them matter.

Thanks to my mom for rescuing Jennifer, the goat, and letting her live in the house until she got strong enough to move into the barn. I was able to write Marvel's story because my mom filled my childhood with unconditional love and a menagerie of animals—dogs and cats, chickens and sheep, horses and goats. These days, she fills my life with laughter, friendship, and, as always, love.

My dad also inspired my love of creatures through trips to the Alligator Farm, his bottomless knowledge of animal facts, and his propensity to rescue things: squirrels, snakes, birds, turtles, and the occasional dog and cat. Even now, he delights me with animal trivia, and I'm lucky to have him in my life.

My sister Angie always makes me smile. Her sweet spirit lifts my heart, and her gentle, carefree ways brighten my life.

My extended family has continued to expand, and I am so happy there is a new crop of littles, London, Maylin, Palmer, and Reef, to enrich our lives with love and happiness.

My own littles, William, Clarice, and Gavin, are teenagers now, but they fill my days with joy and give my life meaning. William's introspection and kindness inspire me to be a better human. Clarice speaks to my soul with her love of books and late-night cups of tea. Gavin warms my heart with his cuddles and laughter. They manage to share me with my fictional characters without *too* much grumbling, even when staring at an empty refrigerator or stepping over piles of laundry.

There are not enough words to express my love for my husband, David. He's built a life for us that I cherish, and I hope he recognizes himself in the pages of this book.

DON'T MISS
THIS MAGICAL ADVENTURE
FROM VICTORIA PIONTEK!

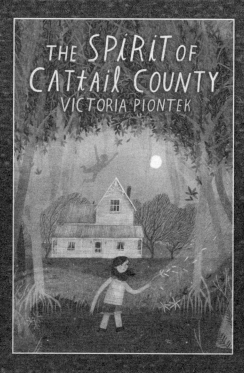

"The two of them had always been different.
She, a girl who looked at death.
He, a ghost who looked like life."

CHAPTER ONE

They buried Sparrow Dalton's mama the day the fortune-teller came. A day so hot, some say the swamp started to bubble. The water of the Everglades rose in the air and hung there, a steaming mist that cloaked the little town of Beulah in a persistent haze.

Sparrow watched as they lowered Mama's casket through the lingering precipitation and into the ground. As the casket creaked and swayed on the ropes that held it fast, vapors swirled in a way that had nothing to do with the weather. Among those rising vapors, Sparrow searched for Mama. She felt with deep certainty she would see Mama again, and she had good reason for this conviction.

Sparrow saw spirits.

In fact, she had seen one ghost, the Boy, with such life-long regularity and clarity that he was as sure as the beat of her young heart.

He was with her even at that moment, as real and as solid as the preacher who presided over Mama's grave. His features were so unlike the murky wisps of typical spirits that she marveled no one else saw him. Though the two of them had always been different. She, a girl who looked at death. He, a ghost who looked like life.

For Sparrow, the only reminder that he was a ghost was his impenetrable silence. He was her greatest secret, yet he told no secrets himself.

She wished he would tell secrets. For if he could talk to her, then it would have been a simple matter to ask after Mama. Sparrow wanted to know where Mama had gone. More important, she wanted to know when Mama would return. Because if the Boy could live side by side with Sparrow, spending long summer days trailing her about the house like a dog, then so could Mama. She knew it wouldn't be exactly as it was before. Sparrow wasn't crazy enough to think that. She only wanted to see Mama again so she wouldn't miss her so much.

Sparrow was so lonely for Mama that her soul ached like a thumping drum, and without Mama, Sparrow had no one to love her.

Sparrow had no sisters, no brothers, and no daddy. Truth be told, she had no true friends either. Sparrow had the misfortune of being an anomaly in a town that took offense at difference. Beulah had never forgiven Sparrow for being born on the same night as the great flood. It seemed folks found it hard to separate her arrival with the rise of the swamp waters. It felt like a bad omen.

To make matters worse, she had the nerve to show up bearing no resemblance to her fair mama. Sparrow had eyes the color of cattails and black hair that twisted like reed grass. Beulah folks joked that Sparrow must be the daughter of the swamp itself to be washed ashore in the flood and so different-looking from Daltons born in generations past. Of course, they wouldn't have speculated so, if Sparrow had a Beulah-born daddy or Mama had stopped the rumors as fast as they'd started. Mama had a defiant streak, though. She'd refused to talk about Sparrow's daddy, and the story stuck.

With Mama gone, Sparrow's only claim to friendship and family were the ghost of a silent boy and Auntie Geraldine, her only living relative.

Sparrow liked the idea of having an aunt. She just didn't like the one she got.

Auntie Geraldine was a force to be reckoned with. A force she applied liberally and often to Sparrow, as she was doing now. Auntie Geraldine pinched the back of Sparrow's arm, for the preacher waited for Sparrow to come forward and cast the first handful of dirt on Mama's grave.

Sparrow had made it clear before they left the house that morning that she wouldn't do this. It was one thing to bury Mama, quite another to throw dirt on her.

Auntie Geraldine smiled up at the preacher and then gave Sparrow another pinch.

Sparrow clamped her hands on the sides of her chair and looked resolutely at the horizon.

A few awkward seconds passed, during which the preacher mopped the sweat from his brow with a hanky and Auntie Geraldine looked around with a forced smile.

Finally, the preacher said, in an overly indulgent and patient way, "Perhaps, sister, you can take her place."

Auntie Geraldine gave an assuring nod and rose, her thin, bony body as strong as steel. She straightened her starched skirt. Paused. Then looked at Sparrow.

She reached out, cupped Sparrow's chin in her hand, and pressed her nails into the tender skin of Sparrow's cheeks before turning to do the preacher's bidding. Auntie Geraldine was good at many things, but was at her best when keeping up appearances.

Auntie Geraldine grabbed a handful of freshly turned soil and held it in her palm. The Boy moved so close to Auntie Geraldine that they were almost touching, and bent down. He put his mouth right next to her palm, as if he would kiss it, and blew. The soil lifted on a ghostly breeze, swirled playfully in the air, and fell like raindrops to the ground.

Auntie Geraldine glared at Sparrow.

It was almost as if she suspected it was Sparrow's fault.

Sparrow glared back, unjustly accused.

She no more controlled the Boy than she did the weather, although she was grateful to him. She hadn't wanted to throw dirt on top of Mama, and now she realized she hadn't wanted anyone else to do it either. Somehow, the Boy knew it. So maybe, in a way, she did control him.

Most likely not. Spirits are fickle things.

ABOUT THE AUTHOR

Victoria Piontek is the author of *The Spirit of Cattail County*, a Bank Street College of Education's Best Children's Book of the Year and a Children's Sequoyah Masterlist selection. As a kid, she was lucky to have a menagerie of pets, including a goat that liked to follow her to the school bus each morning. When she's not writing, you can find her hiking in the Bay Area, where she lives with her husband, three children, and a gigantic fluffy dog. *Better with Butter* is her second novel.